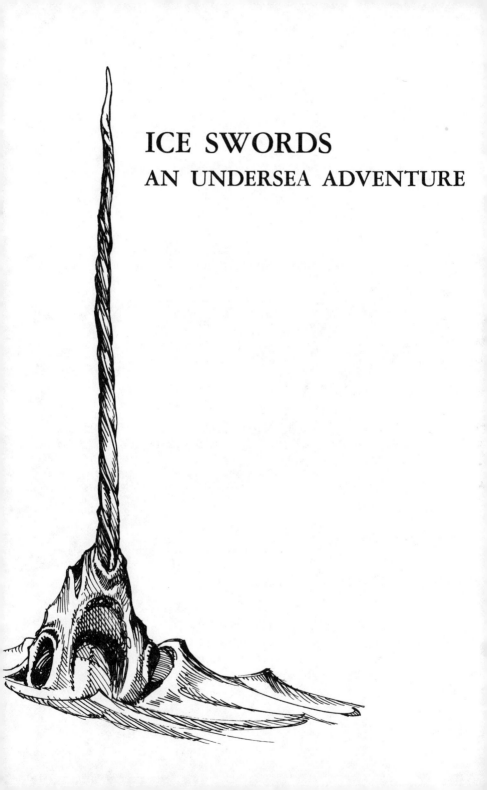

ICE SWORDS
AN UNDERSEA ADVENTURE

ICE SWORDS

AN UNDERSEA ADVENTURE

by James Houston
drawings by the author

A MARGARET K. MC ELDERRY BOOK

Atheneum / 1985 / New York

Library of Congress Cataloging in Publication Data

Houston, James A.,
    Ice swords.

    "A Margaret K. McElderry book."
    Summary: Two boys spending a summer at a research
station in the Arctic to study the migration of whales
learn deep sea diving and encounter dangerous adventure.
    [1. Diving, Submarine—Fiction.   2. Arctic regions—
Fiction.   3. Whales—Fiction]   I. Title.
    PZ7.H819Ic 1985   [Fic]   85–7328
    ISBN 0–689–50333–4

J
Houston
Cp 1

To my wife,
ALICE,
who supports me
in every way

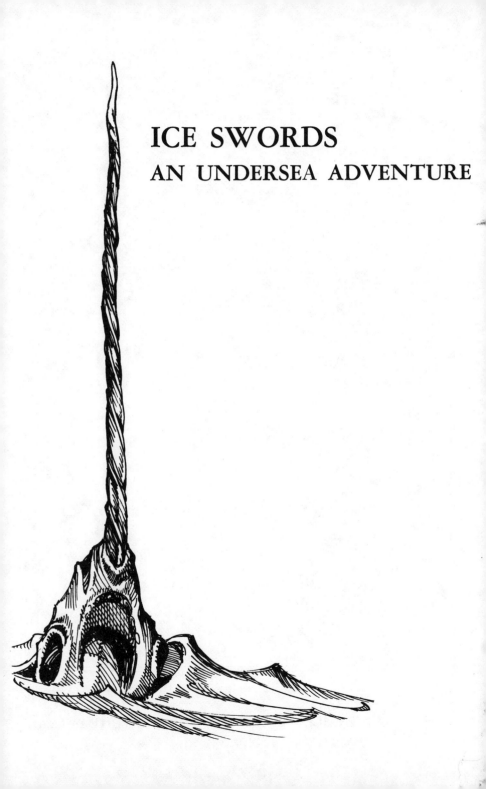

ICE SWORDS
AN UNDERSEA ADVENTURE

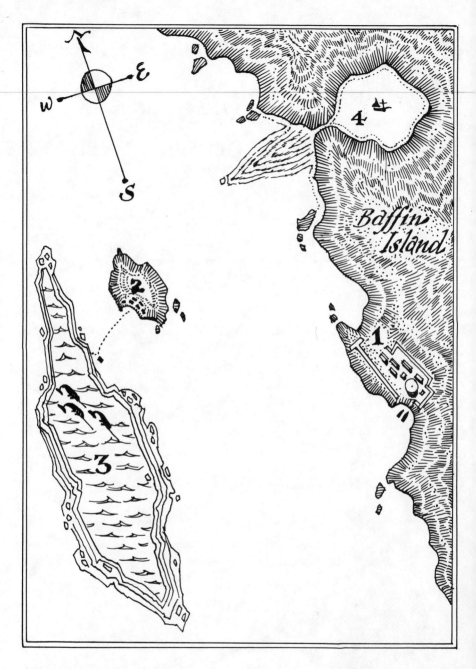

1. DEW LINE FOX FIVE

2. WHALE ISLAND

3. OPENING IN THE ICE

4. WHITE TAIL LAKE

I

"IF WE SURPRISE THEM, WILL THEY ATTACK?" MATTHEW
Morgan asked his best friend, Kayak.

"I don't know," Kayak answered. "These look like
the snowhouses of ancient Tunik people. There are
hunters who may be inside these igloos, waiting
quietly for us with knives and harpoons. Stay behind
me," Kayak whispered. "I'll find out. *Pudluriakpusi*,
we have come visiting," he called into the first igloo
tunnel.

There was no answer from inside, only the icy
Arctic silence that hung all around them.

"Your wild Tunik people make me nervous," said
Charlie, the helicopter pilot, bending to mumble
into Kayak's ear.

There was still no sound from inside any of the
three newly-built igloos.

3

"You leave that rifle standing upright in the snow," Kayak whispered to Matthew, "so we won't frighten them. Then follow me."

Stooping, the two boys made their way through the low snow porch past three dead seals that lay belly up, their hides coated with silver frost.

First Kayak, then Matthew stood upright beneath the glistening igloo dome. The stone seal-oil lamp, burning low, cast weird flickering shadows around the sparkling white walls. No one was inside.

"They were all living here a little while ago," said Matthew. "They must have run away when they heard the oil well explode."

"Look at this, Mattoosie," Kayak said in awe as he picked up a strange stone knife and an arrow-straightener fashioned from caribou antler from the Tunik sleeping bench. "My people in the Arctic haven't used these kinds of hunting tools since my grandfather was young. Look at that ivory harpoon shaft with a sharp stone tip and that curved bow bound with sinew. There is not one thing from the traders in this igloo. No wool blankets, only caribou-skin robes. No iron pots, no rifles. This place makes me kind of jumpy," Kayak whispered. "It belongs to Eskimo people from a long time ago." Kayak was an Inuit who had grown up on Baffin Island near the military air base on the shores of Frobisher Bay.

Kayak and Matthew hurried outside and joined the others.

"You two look as if you have just seen ghosts," said Charlie.

"We did—almost," answered Kayak.

"Not ghosts," said Matthew, pointing. "There they are. Three of them with spears, staring at us from that hill."

"Who are they?" Matt's father asked.

"They look like old-fashioned Tunik to me," Kayak answered. "They are older hunters my folks thought disappeared before my grandfather was born. He told me all about them. These must be the very last of those wild, shy Eskimos. They live in lonely places and never trade with whites. They have no radios, no rifles, no flashlights, no gasoline, no snow-mobiles. They're supposed to be afraid of anything like that. But they still have big fast dog teams, and they are strong and very good at hunting. It is said that long ago we chased them out of our part of the country. That was before your traders came and settled on our island."

"Will those spearmen be afraid of us?" asked Matthew.

"Never," said Kayak. "You are looking at three tough, strong hunters. We won't frighten them away. Wait here. I am going to try to speak to them, ask them if they'll help us get north to Igloolik before we starve."

The others watched as Kayak walked slowly across the snow to greet the Tunik hunters. Partway there he stopped and made an old-fashioned greeting that he must have learned from his grandfather. He pulled off his mitts and raised his hands to prove that he concealed no weapons.

The crouching Tunik hunters whispered among themselves, then rose and, leaving their spears, started to move cautiously toward Kayak. Matt could see that his Inuit friend was tense with excitement.

Then, suddenly, they all heard a loud buzzing in the sky. Everyone turned—to see an airplane diving down straight toward them. The plane's twin engines roared as it swept over them like a fat silver bullet.

The Tunik hunters stared up in terror at the diving plane, then ran back, snatched up their spears, and flung them at the magic bird before they ducked their heads in panic and ran behind the hill.

Kayak raised his hands in despair. "I told you they would never be afraid of us," he called out, "but I didn't say they wouldn't be scared of a *tingmiuk*, a birdlike flying machine."

The heavy cargo plane circled and came lumbering back at them across the sky with a sound like rolling thunder.

Kayak and the others, whose oil-drilling camp had blown up the day before, shaded their eyes against the Arctic glare. They saw that the plane had its wing flaps down for a landing.

"What could be better?" Matt's father shouted. "That's an Air Force plane. The search-and-rescue pilot has spotted our burned-out camp and the wreckage of Charlie's helicopter, *Waltzing Matilda*. He could see our drilling rig and the scorch marks on the snow from the dynamite blast over our blown-out oil well."

"They scared away my Tunik people," Kayak said. said.

"That's true," agreed Matt's father, "but the good news is, the plane is coming in to rescue us."

"Why is it," Matt asked his father, "whenever you and I try to go to some new place, we always have to be rescued? Why can't we rescue ourselves just once, or even rescue other people? Why do we always have to be the ones to get into trouble?"

"Forget that," said his father. "Just you be glad that the Air Force found us. We don't need any more troubles than we've got." Matt's father raised his powerful arms and waved his bandaged hands to the pilot. "Let me tell you one thing, son. If a person wants to be absolutely safe, he can stay at home in a town in bed. But if you want to accomplish something in this world, you have to get out and take real risks."

"Your dad's dead right," said Charlie, as he limped across the snow. "Nothing comes easy in the Arctic. But with a little bit of luck a man could strike it rich up here."

"That plane must have seen the red markers on our landing area. They'll land there on the snow-covered ice of the fish lake," Kayak shouted, as he started running.

"Kayak's using his old beano," shouted Charlie. "Let's go!"

Running and hobbling, the four of them, looking like bandaged scarecrows, stumbled across the snowdrifts. When the plane circled back once more, it seemed so loud and flew so low that Kayak and Matthew ducked their heads in fright.

"I don't blame those Tunik families for being afraid of a noisy bird like that," said Kayak. "Those hunters will harness up their dog teams and run far away from here."

"It's too late to change that now," said Mr. Morgan.

"I guess so," said Kayak, holding his hands over his ears. "But, oh, how I wish that I had got to know them even just a little bit. . . ."

Kayak never finished what he was about to say, for at that moment the big ski-wheel aircraft touched down, kicking up powdery crystals on the hard-snow surface of the frozen lake. The plane swung around on its skis and slid smoothly toward them in the clear bitter cold of the late spring afternoon.

"Four-twenty-nine," said Charlie, looking at his Air Force wristwatch. "I'd want to put that landing time in my log, but I guess it's burned up inside *Matilda*."

"Never mind *Matilda* or the time," Matt's father shouted. "Just be grateful that the Air Force found us."

Charlie flung back his parka hood, revealing his shock of singed red hair. "Look at me! I'm jumping up and down with joy." Charlie laughed. "But let me warn you, that pilot will be in one helluva hurry to pick us up and get that DC-3 out of here. The temperature is really cold. He won't want to shut his engines down. We should send these two lads on the run to bring Professor Volks."

"We'll get him," Kayak and Matthew shouted, as they hurried toward their smoke-blackened Arctic tent.

"He should be able to walk between the two of you," Matt's father called to them. "Be sure he's warmly dressed, and bring his instrument cases. Forget all the rest. Probably we'll just have to leave everything where it lies forever."

When Matt unzipped the front flap of the nylon tent, the professor was already sitting up in his sleeping bag. He looked confused, as if he were in the middle of a dream.

"Did you hear the Air Force rescue plane?" asked Kayak.

"Hear it? *Ja, ja wohl!* It was so low." Professor Volk's eyes widened. "I thought it was going to fly through this tent."

"We are leaving now," said Matt. "We've come to help you to the plane."

"Charlie says the pilot will want to take off quick," Kayak explained.

"*Ich verstehe*, I understand," said the professor, as they unzipped his bag and helped him to his feet. "It's so cold in here it makes my thoughts all go to sleep."

"We'll wrap your sleeping bag around you."

"Pull it over my head, boys." The professor chuckled. "I don't wish to freeze the brains."

Dr. Volks was a small man with a large, balding head. He was a brilliant engineer who, some said, knew more about the science of drilling wildcat oil wells than any other human in the world. He had been flown to this spot on Prince Charles Island in the high Arctic to help with their oil discovery, bringing with him his famous drilling machine named Hansel. It, too, had been severely burned in the oil-well fire.

Matt and Kayak gathered the professor's leather cases, which had not been ruined, and all four sleeping bags. Then, one on each side, supporting the professor, they walked toward the waiting plane.

The two boys did not look at all alike. Mattoosie, as Kayak called his best friend Matt, was tall, with lean, narrow hips and widening shoulders. Like his father, he had big hands and feet, which his body would soon grow to match. He had sandy-colored hair and clear gray eyes and some freckles across his well-formed nose. He was often serious and sometimes sad. That was because four years ago he had lost his mother in a car crash in Arizona. Since that time, Matt had moved to half a dozen different places where his father prospected for metals—to Brazil and Chile, then to Mexico, British Columbia, and Newfoundland. In each place Matt had attended different schools. Because of their many moves, he had made few real friends.

Matt had first known Kayak in the same class at school in Frobisher, and they had soon become like brothers. Kayak had never been south of the Arctic and had never seen a tree except in pictures. He was the son of a clever Eskimo hunter. He was short and handsome, with wide cheekbones, square white teeth, and a smooth, tanned face. He had learned a hundred things that only Inuit hunters know—wise ways to stalk game, to catch birds and fish, and to gauge the weather—Arctic knowledge that ordinary pupils would never learn in school.

"Isn't this very cold for the middle of April?" Professor Volks asked Kayak, as he shuffled forward, wrapped in his sleeping bag.

"Not so bad," said Kayak. "Look at the way the sun is breaking through those heavy snow clouds and lighting up their edges. Oh, sometimes it's a little chilly around here," he admitted, "but my people call this *nunatchiak*. That means it's the most beautiful country in the world."

As soon as they reached the search-and-rescue plane, the pilot revved up the engines. The co-pilot swung open the rear cargo door of the military DC-3, often called "the workhorse of the North." Charlie and Mr. Morgan jumped down onto the snow with a canvas stretcher. The professor seemed relieved to lie down on it, and they eased the stretcher into the plane. When that was done, the pilot and copilot, who both wore bulky fur hats and thickly-padded coveralls, slammed and bolted the metal door. They wrapped the professor's sleeping bag around him once more, then fastened down the stretcher with three special belts.

"Find a seat and buckle up," the pilot called to the rest of them. The plane bumped along the low drifts at the far end of the lake, then swung into the wind and roared back across the smooth, snow-covered ice. The aircraft's skis hit one hard snowdrift, and the plane lurched into the air.

Looking out the window, Kayak could, for a minute, see *Waltzing Matilda* tipped over on the snow like a burned and broken toy. Slowly, their red nylon tent, the fire-blackened tractor, and their dynamite-blasted oil well disappeared. Their search for black diamonds, as oil was nicknamed, had ended.

Matthew lay back. This was the first moment since the explosion that he had a chance to think calmly of the terrible events that had nearly killed all of them. The worst part was when he and Kayak had been slipping helplessly toward the edge of a cliff with a box of dynamite. Below, they could see the flaming oil well onto which they would fall. Was it possible that a pair of hands had reached out and saved them?

Matt closed his eyes as he remembered the awful blast when the oil well exploded and the terror he had felt as he searched among the searing-hot rocks for his father and Kayak and Charlie and the professor, all cut and bruised by flying rocks and with heat-blistered hands and faces, but by a miracle, all were still alive. He thought again of his new fear that had surfaced as the Arctic cold seeped back around them after the fire burned out. Painfully they had gathered together their charred sleeping bags and crowded into the one remaining tent, lit two candles, and survived the night.

Remembering the horrors of yesterday and today

—until they discovered the Tunik hunters who then fled from the rescue plane—Matthew fell asleep. He jerked awake when the copilot touched his shoulder. The airman poured some lukewarm coffee from a big steel thermos and offered Matt a choice of soggy sandwiches that had been made days before at an air base in southern Canada .

"This is some lucky day for us," the copilot said, smiling. "Imagine us finding your wildcat drilling operation in the middle of nowhere. Happy coffee hour!"

The copilot looked over at the professor, whose face was very pale. "There is no doctor at Foxe Five, but there may be a military medic. The pilot has asked them to light up their runway. We have to go in there and refuel."

"What is Foxe Five?" Matthew asked, but the copilot, already heading for his seat, didn't hear him over the noisy engine roar.

"Foxe Five," Charlie answered, "is the code name for a DEW Line site. *DEW* means Defense Early Warning. Together the U.S. and Canada built listen-posts in the Arctic across Alaska and Canada to Greenland. Foxe Five is one of those sites that would warn us if a missile attack came across the pole." He yawned and looked at his wristwatch. "I hope we'll be there in time for dinner. I'm hungry as a duck-billed platypus."

"I'm starving, too," said Matt.

His father laughed. "That's normal for a fourteen-year-old boy who's growing faster than a Scottish thistle."

"The pilot's got a compass fix on Foxe Five now." The co-pilot pointed. "You can see the airstrip lights off there to the east."

When they landed, the copilot came back into the body of the plane. "We'll stay here tonight," he explained. "If the weather's right, tomorrow morning early we'll fly south to Churchill, then on to Winnipeg, Manitoba."

"Winnipeg?" said Charlie. "That's great for the professor. It will get him into hospital."

Matt saw his father slump. "But Winnipeg's two thousand miles south. That's no good at all for us. We want to fly east to Frobisher on Baffin Island. We've got to stay in the Arctic until our oil leases are cleared, and we've got to check out our insurance and try to find someone to help salvage Charie's helicopter."

The copilot undid the professor's seat belts and grasped one end of the stretcher. The Foxe Five medic hopped aboard and took the other. Professor Volks was still dazed but managed a faint smile as they placed him gently in the heated cab of a snow tractor, large enough to carry all of them. They made a fast, smooth ride to the main building of Foxe Five.

When they were inside the brightly lighted entrance hall, they stripped off their outer boots, wind pants, and parkas.

"Oh, it's big in here—and hot," said Kayak.

"And too much light." Matt blinked his eyes. "But they must have a good cook. Smell that food. Roasting meat, cooked vegetables, and fresh-baked apple pie!"

After showing them three rooms where they could sleep, Archibald McKenzie, the manager of Foxe Five, led them to the large mess hall. "The Air Force will fly the professor to the hospital in Winnipeg," he said. "The only other plane leaving tomorrow belongs to the Royal Canadian Mounted Police. This is its pilot, Sergeant Beaumont. This is Ross Morgan, and you know Charlie. And this is Kayak and Matthew Morgan."

Matt and Kayak shook hands with the pilot.

"These four have to get back to Frobisher. Could you arrange a lift for them?" said Archibald Mc-Kenzie.

Sergeant Beaumont shook his head. "I've got orders to take three men from this site and also a pile of freight. I guess I could manage to take two of you, if you bring nothing heavier than your toothbrushes."

Ross Morgan looked at his son and then at Kayak. "We can't just leave you here," he said.

"Why not?" Matthew asked. "It's safe here for us, and anyway we couldn't help you with the work that you and Charlie have to do."

"We don't mind staying here," said Kayak. "It's interesting. I don't know anyone at school who has been on a DEW Line site. Not even our teacher."

"The boys are right," Mr. McKenzie agreed. "They would be just as well off inside these buildings as anywhere on earth: good food, warm beds, Ping-Pong tables, fairly new magazines, and a movie once a week."

"We want to stay," said Matthew. "Will you let us, Dad?"

"I guess I've got no other choice."

Charlie laughed. "You might say these two lads are getting nature's wild and woolly schooling in the north instead of a proper education. That's the way lots of my chums did it in the Outback of Australia. Some learned to hop about like kangaroos and throw a ruddy boomerang before they could add up three and seven. Mind you, a few of them turned into sheep ranching millionaires."

"What's a ruddy boom-moor-oongg?" asked Kayak.

"A boomerang is long as your arm and flat like a helicopter blade, but bent," said Charlie. "The native Outback people can teach you how to throw it so it comes flying back to you. It'll knick off your ear, if you don't duck fast."

"Well, is that settled?" Sergeant Beaumont asked. "Ross Morgan and Charlie fly to Frobisher with me, and these two lucky lads stay here until you two get back."

"Right!" said Mr. Morgan. "That's how it's got to be."

Charlie added, "Those two know how to take care of themselves." He reached out and clapped Kayak and Matt on the back. Charlie was always cheerful, always full of hope.

"Mattoosie, are all Australians as good as Charlie?" Kayak asked, when they went back to get another helping of apple pie.

"Sure, Australians are good," Matthew told him, "but Charlie, well, he's special. Did you see him trying to smile when the medic here was changing his bandages? And he knows his helicopter, *Waltzing Matilda*, is probably ruined, but you don't hear him giving up."

The two boys rose early next morning to say good-bye to the professor and help him aboard the plane.

"He's a very special person," said Kayak. "He asked us to visit him in Germany when he gets better. I'd like to do that."

After breakfast, when it was time for the Mounted Police plane to leave, Matt and his father felt shy because of the dozens of men who were looking on, so they turned their usual hug into a manly handshake. Charlie and Kayak weren't shy. They flung a bear hug around each other and danced a farewell jig.

Charlie called out in a hearty voice, "Kayak, I'll drop in and visit your family and tell them you look pretty good to me."

"Thanks, and if you see our teacher," Kayak said, "tell her Mattoosie and I aren't just playing hooky. We couldn't come to school because of lots of troubles with oil wells burning, dynamite blowing up on us, and *Waltzing Matilda* getting—"

"I'll tell her, and don't you go worrying about the

old waltzer." Charlie paused for a moment. "She's a tough old wallaby. She'll fly again, you'll see."

Mr. McKenzie joined Matt and Kayak on the airstrip. They pulled up their parka hoods when Sergeant Beaumont roared his engines and sent a great snow blizzard billowing out toward them. The plane rose, cutting sharply through the clear blue Arctic sky. They watched until it disappeared.

Mr. McKenzie gave the boys a fast ride back to the high wire gate. When Matt got out to open it, he saw a large red-lettered sign. It read:

DANGER
POLAR BEARS FREQUENTLY WANDER
AMONG THESE BUILDINGS SEARCHING FOR FOOD.
MEN OUT WALKING MUST CARRY A RIFLE.

"I don't like the sound of that," said Matthew, as he jumped inside the Snowcat and quickly slammed the door. "I don't like bears coming close to me."

That morning, Mr. McKenzie took them around and showed them everything that wasn't supersecret. The DEW Line base was situated not far from shore, where the sea ice stretched endlessly to a small island. Beyond that a dark streak of open water threw up a cold black fog on the horizon. The largest building on the base was a strange, round geodesic dome that looked like an enormous golf ball. No visitors were allowed inside it.

"Kayak, would you like to live here?" Matthew asked after Mr. McKenzie had gone.

"Not me," said Kayak. "I'd rather live in an igloo like those Tunik hunters or in a tent that is easy to move. This place is too big and slow for me. I like to travel, move around. I like moving with the animals."

"I know," said Matthew, "but don't you enjoy going through the door at mealtime and smelling all that wonderful food the cook has made?"

"You've been hungry for too long, Mattoosie. We can't just eat and sleep all day and make noises like Igtuk the Boomer."

"Who's Igtuk the Boomer?" Matthew asked.

"Oh, he's the mountain spirit, very noisy, always hungry. They say he eats everything, even stones."

For the rest of that morning, Matt and Kayak played fast and furious Ping-Pong. Matthew was the first to toss his paddle on the wide green table. He was not surprised, for he already knew how strong and tireless his adopted brother was. Kayak had a short neck and powerful arms, with a deep chest and sloping shoulders. He was fifteen years old and, though he had short legs, he could run faster than any boy in school except Matthew. But when it came to running on loose snow, Matthew knew that he could never catch up with Kayak.

Kayak had loved and admired his grandfather, who had tried to teach him all he knew before he died. This knowledge of the animals and the sea and land Kayak used when he went off hunting with his father in the summer. And he had used it when he and Matthew had tried desperately to get back to Frobisher after the long search they had made for Charlie and Matt's father, who had failed to come back from a prospecting trip a year ago.

Kayak had told Matthew about his grandfather and had proudly shown him the buckhorn-handled knife, one of the few things his grandfather possessed, that the old man had left him. It was one of the first knives ever traded by the Hudson's Bay Company when they established their earliest post on south Baffin Island. The knife's steel blade was worn narrow from many sharpenings, but there was no other knife like it. It was Kayak's most treasured possession, along with his big dog, Shulu.

"Let's go for a run," Matthew suggested after lunch.

Remembering the red sign that warned them of polar bears, Kayak took down one of the heavy rifles that hung near the door and put a flat box of ammunition in his pocket.

"Bears can smell meat from a long way off," Kayak said. "I think they gather here because of the good cooking."

"Listen!" said Matt, when they stopped outside. "What's that noise?"

Kayak pointed out toward the sea ice at two snowmobiles. "That purple one is driven by an Inuk, Eskimo-style. I can tell because it's going faster and a little smoother over the snowdrifts than the other one, which must be driven by a *kaluna,* a white man."

When the two snowmobiles roared toward them, Matt could see that Kayak's guess was right. They waved at the two men, who waved back before they halted their Skidoos in front of the mess-hall door.

"I wonder," Kayak said, "what those two were doing on the sea ice. There's nothing I can see out there but that one faraway island."

"*Kunowepeet.*" The strong-looking Eskimo man smiled and shook hands with both boys.

Back in the building, Kayak returned the rifle and the ammunition to the rack.

"My name's Kayak," he said in Inuktitut, using the Eskimo language. "I'm from Ikhaloweet," he added, using the native word for Frobisher. "And this is my best friend, Mattoosie. I've taken him as my brother."

"My name is Ashevak," the Eskimo answered, speaking English. "I'm down here from Igloolik. And this is my friend, Dr. Sandy Lunan." He drew out the last name, long and slow—Looon-annn. "He can dive underwater like a loon. That's why the Inuit call him Tudlik. That means loon. We have come in from Whale Island."

The white man reached out and shook hands strangely. He was of medium height with steady gray eyes, light brown hair, and a wide smile that made Matt know they'd like him. Ashevak, who stood beside him, had to help him take off his parka, and when he did, the boys saw that his right arm was in a plaster cast.

"Fell and broke it on the ice," said Dr. Lunan. "Oh, it's getting better, but it has ruined my diving time up here. I was given a grant from the San Diego

Ocean Mammal Program, but with this broken flipper, I'll never get my work completed. I've sent the other divers who came north with me down to Tikirak, near Cape Dorset, to study the walrus feeding habits. That leaves Ashevak and me to report here on the spring whale migration. We only came in from our research station because I'm expecting a couple of messages from the south, and our radio's been acting up on us."

Ashevak saw the DEW Line operator hurrying across the mess hall with some papers in his hand.

Because of his broken arm, Dr. Lunan tore open the first message with his teeth. He read it aloud so they could hear.

"Dr. Sanderson Lunan
Arctic Experimental Station
North Baffin Island, N.W.T. Canada
Your sea mammal observation project must be completed by August 1. No monies, repeat, no monies, available beyond that date. Good Luck, Signed,

The Director"

"That's the bad news. Now, let's hope this one is good news. It's a night letter." He tore it open in the same way.

"Dearest Sandy:
Alarmed to hear of your compound fracture. Afraid it will hamper your project. Jill insists on going

north with diving gear to help you. She leaves San Diego on night plane. Take good care of yourself and Jill.

> Your loving wife,
> Elizabeth"

"Well, I'll be glad to see her, but I don't know what possible good Jill—my daughter—can do up here," said Sandy Lunan. "I can't dive with her, and I wouldn't want her to go under the ice all by herself."

"I wouldn't let me *or* my daughter go under any ice," said Ashevak.

Kayak and Ashevak drained their coffee cups as they talked softly together in their own language.

"Mattoosie, you want to know what we're saying? We're talking about *akbil*—big whales—*kilaloak*—white whales—*agalingwak*—narwhals, all different kinds of whales. Ashevak hopes we can visit Whale Island with them and see their diving station. The narwhal migration hasn't arrived yet. These two men, they're waiting and watching for the *agalingwak* every day."

"I'd like to go and see that place," said Matthew.

"You two are more than welcome to come out and stay with us," said Dr. Lunan. "Here comes Archie McKenzie. We can aks him if it would be all right if you came visiting for a few days. Ashevak's wife and daughter are there. We'll all be glad of some extra company."

"Sure, you can go," said Mr. McKenzie. "I know your dad won't mind. You'll be learning something useful. Soon as we hear from him, I'll let you know."

The radio operator interrupted them. "Dr. Lunan, we've got a third message for you from Polar Airways. It says Buzzer met the jet at Resolute, and instead of bringing your daughter to Foxe Five, he will use the emergency strip at Whale Island. He should be there about 1600 hours."

Sandy Lunan looked at his wristwatch. "That's four o'clock. We've got to hurry."

The two boys ran along the hall to their bedrooms, gathered up their sleeping bags, rushed out, and tied them on the small sled behind Ashevak's snowmobile.

"We'll race you!" Kayak shouted, as he jumped on the seat behind Ashevak.

"Oh, no, we won't," said Ashevak. "Dr. Lunan's got a broken arm. He's not supposed to race with only one hand on the controls. He's going to go nice and slow, aren't you, Dr. Lunan?"

Matt pulled up his parka hood and tied his woolen scarf over his mouth and nose. He sat in back of Dr. Lunan, who started up the engine of his green snowmobile and meekly followed in Ashevak's blue-shadowed tracks.

They were no sooner out on the snow-covered sea ice than Dr. Lunan seemed to tire of going slowly, and he roared his Skidoo up beside Ashevak, who was trying to wave him back. Soon the two of them were laughing and racing each other, trying to beat the wind as they rushed toward Whale Island. Matt and Kayak held on tight.

"Hurry!" shouted Sandy Lunan. "We want to be right there when my daughter Jill comes hopping off that plane."

II

"THERE'S BUZZER NOW!" DR. LUNAN SHOUTED, POINTING to a dot in the sky no bigger than a mosquito that was growing larger. "Come on, boys. Jill must be with him. Let's go and meet them."

Both men gunned their engines as a small, single-engine plane came sloping in for a landing. Using his one good arm, Sandy Lunan turned his snowmobile in a fast, wide curve. He and Matthew raced Ashevak and Kayak across the snow-packed ice toward the bright-orange air sock marking a hard-snow strip for aircraft landings. The pilot skillfully jockeyed his airplane along the strip on its stubby skis, stopping close enough for Matthew to reach out and touch its wing tip.

Buzzer cut the engine and flung open his side door. "Here she is, Sandy," called the bush pilot in a booming voice. "One very useful daughter, delivered safe and sound."

Without the plane's roaring engine or the grinding clatter of the snowmobiles, the utter silence of the Arctic seemed to leave them speechless.

Buzzer reached across the little cabin and pushed Jill's door open. She undid her seat belt, struggled stiffly out beneath the wing, slipped from the metal step, and fell flat on the snow. Ashevak leaped forward and politely helped her to her feet.

"Mattoosie, that can't be a real girl," Kayak whispered to his friend. "She's too long to be a girl."

"Oh, she's a girl all right," Matthew answered into Kayak's ear. "They grow them tall in California. But I never saw one dressed like that before."

Jill Lunan was wearing a curious mixture of everything warm that she had been able to find in the San Diego stores, where they were aready featuring swimsuits for the spring season. Beneath a bright wool coat, her dark-blue ski pants smoothly disappeared inside an enormous pair of sheepskin boots of the kind that Sherpa guides in northern India wear when they're off the mountains, relaxing around a fire. She wore a bright wool hat and the mitts of a Lapland reindeer herder.

Jill pulled off those mitts, then her inner mitts and gloves, and removed the huge dark glasses that almost hid her face. She hugged her father and smiled when she shook hands with all of them. Kayak noticed that she was smoothly tanned and had perfect teeth.

Sandy Lunan beamed at his daughter and, using his good left arm, gave her a second hug. Then turning proudly to the others, he said, "My Jill's a first-class diver, sleek as a salmon when she's underwater. But I hope you three will help me take good care of her on land. Only in these last few days has Jill ever put her foot on snow."

"Oh, Dad!" Jill groaned, and her cheeks flushed red. "I'm going to be sixteen soon. I don't need that much caring for. I've come here to help you with the diving. You've got a broken arm. Remember? Mom sends you all her love and says you should send her a radio message as soon as I arrive."

"She sounds like a girl," Kayak whispered. "I like her eyes without those sunglasses and the way she smiles."

Buzzer handed Jill her backpack from the plane. Dangling from the outside hung a pair of goggles and a froglike pair of diver's fins.

When he saw the fins, Jill's father shook his head. "I haven't had a pair of those on my feet for over a month. I've done nothing but sit around here like a fish out of water, staring at this broken flipper of mine and listening to our underwater microphones, knowing that our narwhal study grant is running out on us."

"Too bad," said Buzzer, as he tossed Jill's other baggage down onto the snow.

"That's a girl, all right," Matthew whispered. "Just look at all the stuff she's brought up here with her.

Probably perfumes and shampoos, makeup kits, and a big hair dryer, and purple ballet slippers."

"Whatever she's got in these bags," said Kayak, as he picked one up, "it's very, very *ohohmitoalook*. That means heavy! But I'll bet she could carry it all." He looked at Jill and then at Matt. "She's about the same size as you."

"Jill can share my tent with me," her father said, "and you two boys are welcome to use that other double tent for as long as you stay out here. It cheers my heart to have a couple of extra whaling students with us on this island." He pointed out beyond the sea ice to the blackness of the open water. "The spring narwhal migration should pass near here sometime soon. That means we'll have to keep a constant watch."

"I'm going to take off now while the engine's warm and the weather's good," said Buzzer. "If I stayed the night, I might scare your narwhals in the morning."

"I doubt they'll be here that soon. Thanks for bringing Jill," said Sandy Lunan.

Buzzer waved, then gunned the engine, ran his small plane down the flat snow strip, and rose into the air, They piled Jill's luggage on her father's snowmobile and drove it—more slowly this time— back to Dr. Lunan's tent. Ashevak's wife, Uvilu, and his daughter, Susee, greeted Jill and Matt and Kayak warmly in Inuktitut.

Jill looked at her father's research station: a collection of half a dozen red-nylon tents, a tall, thin radio mast, and the one collapsible plywood building, painted blue, that was about the size of a double garage. Yellow tarpaulins covered numerous piles of supplies, and beside the cook tent were two sturdy upturned rowboats and an Eskimo dogsled.

When Kayak and Matthew had lugged her baggage into her father's tent, Jill said, "Will you two help me hang up all this stuff?"

She unzipped the largest canvas bag and pulled out two bulky rubber wet suits for diving—one red, one green—and two pairs of extra black swimming fins, three face masks, a spear gun, a wicked-looking diver's knife, and something else she called a "bang stick," three suits of long woolen underwear, rubber gloves, two inflatable life jackets, and one thin coil of yellow-nylon rope.

"She doesn't have any purple shoes or hair dryer or mirrors that I can see," said Kayak, when he and Matt unrolled their sleeping bags in their own tent a bit later. "But she's got all the things she needs for hunting underwater .That second, green rubber suit would probably fit you, Mattoosie."

"I suppose you're right," said Matt. "I guess I was kind of wrong about this girl bringing a lot of silly stuff with her."

When Jill entered the kitchen tent to help Ashevak's wife make dinner, Kayak and Matthew were surprised by what they saw. She now wore blue jeans and a dark-blue turtleneck sweater. Her light-brown hair was drawn neatly back and tied in a ponytail.

Also, she had on knee-high Apache moccasins with large silver studs.

"Are those boots from Ari-zoo-na?" Kayak asked her.

"They are, indeed," said Jill. "How did you know that?"

"I saw a picture of them in a book," said Kayak. "It was the same Indians who taught Mattoosie to do a clever signal trick with a mirror. That trick helped save our lives."

"Did you ever live in Arizona?" Matthew asked Jill.

"No, I've always lived near San Diego, but I've visited my aunt there, in Tucson. I've traveled to quite a few places. That's because my dad is a biologist, always studying some kind of whale—in Hawaii or Norway or off the coast of South America."

"My dad's like that, too," said Matthew. "He's a geologist, and a high-school teacher sometimes, always hunting for gold or copper, oil or silver, somewhere, anywhere in the world."

"My dad's a hunter, too," said Kayak. "He hunts seals and caribou to feed our family. So that makes the three of us all the kids of hunters. It's kind of like being brothers and sisters from far-off places. Right?"

"I like that idea," said Jill. "Why don't you sit down at the table. I'm going to make some hard sauce for this fruitcake my mom had me bring up to Dad because we missed his birthday."

When the meal was over, Ashevak rubbed his stomach and said thanks to Dr. Lunan. "*Aheeaktoopa!* Your daughter's good at making that white stuff."

"Jill's good at lots of things," Sandy Lunan answered proudly. "Wait until you see her underwater. I'd match her against any young diver in the state of California."

"Oh, Dad, I've got lots to learn," Jill exclaimed. "I've never dived in cold water. I'll probably freeze up like a clam. But I can scarcely wait to try it."

"It's not as bad as it looks," said Dr. Lunan, "but you wouldn't want to do it in your bikini. Would you two boys like to learn to dive?"

"I don't know." Matthew shook his head.

"Me, neither," Kayak said. "Mattoosie and I are like real brothers. We do things together, or not at all."

"That's too bad," said Dr. Lunan. "Jill has her instructor's certificate, and she could qualify you both to dive."

"I'd be glad to teach you." Jill smiled. "It shouldn't take too long. I think you'd love diving, when you know how, and—"

Kayak raised his hand. "If you're going to be the schoolteacher, I will come to your class," he said shyly.

"Well," said Matthew, "if Kayak's going to do it, I will, too." He winked at Kayak. "I would hate to miss any school."

"If the weather's good tomorrow around noon," said Sandy Lunan, "you can do a dive, Jill. You'll only understand these Arctic waters after you've tried them. But not under the ice. I won't let you risk that alone. There always must be at least two divers working together underneath the ice. You boys can watch Jill through the small window Ashevak and I have set into the bottom of one of the rowboats."

Next day, it was cold and very clear. At about eleven-thirty in the morning, Jill appeared in the kitchen tent. She was wearing a tight-fitting, cherry-red wet suit, with her father's blue eiderdown jacket flung across her shoulders, and her sheepskin-lined Sherpa boots.

"I'm going to eat a little something now to keep me warm when I go underwater," Jill told them, "but not enough to give me cramps."

"I'll eat some of that leftover turkey bird with you," Kayak said, "so I won't get too cold just seeing you go down there and turn into a frozen fish."

Jill was laughing when Ashevak came in for coffee.

"Your dad and I will go on the first snowmobile," Ashevak told Jill. "We'll haul the rowboat on the sled and set up the diver's tent. Then you three come after us at noon."

Using the other snowmobile, the journey took them only fifteen minutes from their island across the flat, snow-covered ice to the place kept open by the power of the tides. When Kayak, Matt, and Jill arrived at the edge of the solid ice, they saw that the bright-orange diver's tent was up, and the small kerosene stove inside it was causing wisps of steam to seep out of the entrance.

Jill's father showed Ashevak how to strap her air tanks on her back and to check her weighted belt, safety line, life jacket, rubber hood, and last of all, her breathing regulator.

"Only five minutes this first time," said Jill's father. "You check your watch with mine while we attach this safety line to you."

"All you have to do is give three jerks," said Ashevak, "and I will haul you to the surface fast, if . . . well, if . . . you see something down there . . . that you don't like the look of."

Jill sat down on the edge of the ice, then turned and waved at all of them. She gave a quick push out into the water and disappeared.

"Hurry, jump in the boat," said Kayak. "I'm afraid something bad is going to happen to her down there."

Together Matt and Kayak forced the rowboat out into the thick, icy slush.

"I'm kind of scared to even look down," said Kayak. "You look first. I'll row."

Matt crouched on the bottom, peering through the thick eight-inch square of Plexiglas, feeling the icy coldness of the water through the bottom of the boat.

"Can you see her?" Kayak asked Matt.

"No, I can't see her. But I just saw two big jellyfish."

"Never mind the jellyfish," said Kayak. "Where is Jill?"

"Holy smoke! There she is! She's not far down. You can see her very well in that red suit. She's letting out long streams of bubbles. Now she's rolling over and she's waving up at us."

"You're fooling," Kayak said.

"Here, you look at her yourself," said Matthew. "You watch her waving while I do the rowing."

When they changed places, Kayak could see her right away. Jill was looking up at him. She kept rolling over like a sleek, scarlet porpoise, kicking her flippers slowly while she held her arms tight to her sides.

"She's going down," said Kayak. "She's heading for the bottom. Its' getting harder to see her. Oh, she just turned on her light."

Dr. Lunan called, "There is something near Jill. Can you see it?" He was listening to the underwater microphone.

"Let me look again," said Matthew, and he knelt in the middle of the boat. "What's that swimming not too far from her?" he asked.

"Move over," said Kayak, shipping the oars, and he, too, bent and peered through the little window. "It's a *netsiavinik*, a young seal," said Kayak.

"It's going right up to her. It's not at all afraid of her." Matt shook his head in wonder.

"The way it squeaks, it sounds like a ringed seal," called Dr. Lunan.

"You're right," Matthew yelled. "It is a seal."

"Oh, I want to go down there," said Kayak. "That's a whole new world, a whole new way of hunting."

"I can't wait to make a dive," said Matthew. "I

won't mind as long as I have open water overhead. I'm sure I wouldn't like it underneath the ice.' '

"Get ready!" Sandy Lunan called to them. "Jill will be surfacing in fifteen seconds."

Matt pulled hard on his right oar, and the small boat spun around. They touched the edge of the main ice just as Jill's red-hooded head popped above the water's surface. Ashevak pulled off her heavy back tanks, then helped Jill out onto the ice.

"Ittt wa-wa-was greeeaat!" Jill stuttered, as she pushed up her mask. Her lips were blue and her face was pinched and lined like that of an old, old woman. She could not keep herself from shaking.

"I knew you'd find it cold, especially the first time," said her father. "You go warm up in the tent and keep this insulated blanket around yourself. There's a thermos of hot cocoa."

In about ten minutes, Jill came out again. This time her face was smooth and her cheeks were red once more. She was no longer trembling from the cold. Her wet suit was partly unzipped, and Matt could read the word *Navy* on her faded undershirt.

"Oh, Dad, that was a wonderful dive," she said. "Can I go down again tomorrow?"

When they were racing back to camp on the two snowmobiles, Kayak cupped his hand and shouted near Jill's ear. "Will you teach me how to swim? I've never been in the water in my whole life, except once, when I fell out of a boat. My father had to snatch me back or I'd have drowned."

"Swimming's easy," Matt told him. "It's using a

breathing regulator, mask, and air tanks that we both have to learn from Jill."

When they walked into the dining tent, Sandy Lunan was already there.

"Did you say the green wet suit fits Matt?" her father asked.

"Yes," Jill replied. "I had him try it on."

Dr. Lunan got out his tape measure and said, "Well, then, first thing we've got to do is measure you, Kayak, then order you a wet suit. I'll radio Vancouver tonight. They should fly it up within the week."

That night, conditions on the radio were clear and, using new batteries, they were able to contact Foxe Five, whose radio operator relayed their messages to Vancouver and to Frobisher. In no time, Matt was speaking on a phone patch with his father.

"Are you two all right?" Ross Morgan asked.

"We're fine," said Matthew. "We're out on Whale Island, not far from Foxe Five. Dr. Lunan is here with us. He's teaching us a lot about whales."

"Ask your dad to tell our teacher we're back in school," said Kayak. "I don't want her to think we're just playing around having a good time. Tell him to say we've got an awful strict girl teacher here who makes us work too hard."

"I'll tell her," Matt's father said, in reply "Take good care, you two. We'll see you soon. Good night."

When they woke next morning, the air had warmed and gray snow clouds were rolling in from the south-west.

"I don't think you'll be doing any outdoor diving for the next few days," said Ashevak, and he was right.

Dr. Lunan gave them a book on diving that they read together through the day. By evening, when they gathered for dinner, there was a howling ice storm. Later, Jill got out several of her father's slides and showed them photographs of scuba divers swimming in warm, blue waters more than three thousand miles south of Whale Island.

"I've got a bright idea," said Sandy Lunan. "We could set up the green plastic tank that the Fish and Wildlife Service sent up here to use for an aquarium, in case we had the luck to capture a live narwhal. These boys could learn to scuba dive in it."

"That's a great idea," said Jill. "That's where I'll hold my school."

Working together, they erected the green plastic swim tank that was almost as large as the inside of the collapsible plywood shed. When they were finished, Ashevak fitted a hose into a hole cut in the ice and, using a small motor, they pumped the narwhal tank full of salt water. Matt guessed it was about the size of twenty-four bathtubs, just big enough for one narwhal or three humans to swim and dive in.

Four nights later, at eight o'clock, Dr. Lunan made his regular radio contact with Foxe Five. "Two messages on the radio! The first says Kayak's new wet suit arrived safely over at Foxe Five. You two lads can go with Ashevak and pick it up. And the second message is that Matt's dad wants to speak to him on the radio when he gets there."

Next day, when they returned with the wet suit, Matt told Dr. Lunan what his father had reported. "Everything's going very slowly. He's trying to settle oil leases with the government, and Charlie's flown back to our oil drilling site with a good mechanic. They're trying to get poor old *Matilda* in the air again. Dad says he's glad we're going to school and learning about whales. He says we should wait around here until he and Charlie can come and pick us up."

Eagerly they unpacked the new black wet suit. Kayak went and tried it on.

"It fits you perfectly," said Jill. "Tomorrow we'll have our first lesson."

Following the book, she taught them all the items of equipment, surface swimming, regulator breathing, and the shallow dive. "I looked in on you several times today," Sandy Lunan said at dinner that night, "and everything seemed to be going well."

"These two learn fast," Jill told her father. "It won't be very long before they're first-class divers."

"She's a good teacher," Kayak said. "Maybe I'll be the first Inuk ever to go hunting underneath the water." Kayak turned to Ashevak and said, "I wonder if I could throw a harpoon down there?"

"I don't think you could," Ashevak replied, "but you'll have a chance to find that out for yourself."

Suddenly they heard a series of fast clicks and a long, low groan coming from the underwater receiver they had installed.

"What was that?" asked Kayak.

"I don't know," said Dr. Lunan. "It's different from the usual sounds we hear from seals and rock cod." He leaned back and turned up the volume of the receiver.

They listened carefully, but the curious sound from beneath the sea did not come again.

"We've laid wiring to the reefs with underwater microphones," Ashevak explained. "We'll know if whales are out there, even in the dark or fog, by the noises they'll make."

"Was that sound from a whale?" asked Matthew.

Dr. Lunan and Ashevak looked at each other, but they did not answer.

"I hope it's true that even the biggest whales will never try to hurt a diver." Matt looked seriously at Jill's father.

"Mattoosie, don't talk too much about swimming around with whales," said Kayak. "I'm trying to forget about that Bible story with Jonah being swallowed by a great fish."

For six more days and nights, the late spring storm continued, slowly changing from snow to sleet, then cold rain, spreading wide blue lakes across the sea ice. Every day Jill, with her father giving advice from the side, worked with Matt and Kayak, who had quickly become a fine, strong swimmer.

"In one week," said Dr. Lunan, "you two have

learned what it would usually take most beginning divers a month or more to learn. I don't want either you or Jill to dive until this water has warmed up a bit. I don't like to see my divers coming up with their faces blue. If we're lucky, the narwhals won't come for maybe a month, though they may arrive tomorrow. It will be warmer then. Observing whales is a question of patience."

Just as Dr. Lunan finished speaking, they heard an inhuman, high-pitched scream come shrieking out of the underwater receiver.

Kayak leaped up from the table. "What made that noise?"

Even as he spoke, another piercing sound came ripping through the tent, so loud this time it made all of them clap their hands over their ears.

III

"I DON'T KNOW WHAT COULD HAVE MADE A MONSTROUS sound like that," said Dr. Lunan. "It's certainly not a bowhead or a sperm whale."

"Could it have been a narwhal?" Jill asked her father.

"No, no. I don't think so," he said. "I've heard some Danish recordings of narwhals off Greenland. Their sounds are not nearly as violent as this call. I'd say we heard a much larger type of whale."

The unseen creature gave another piercing shriek followed by a long tearing sound.

"It cuts through the water very fast." Sandy Lunan whistled. "Just listen to that ripping sound. For myself, I'd like to see what made that sound, but for the narwhals' sake, I hope it goes away right now. We don't need a fierce thing like that around this island."

During the next few days, they heard nothing from the underwater microphones except the usual squeals of seals and grunts of rock cod. They could not even see the open water, so thickly was it blanketed in summer fog.

In the evening of the fourth day, the fog began to drift away. Ashevak and Dr. Lunan sat together after dinner in the cook tent drinking coffee. Kayak, Jill, and Matt came in and joined them.

"Ashevak," said Jill, "what do you know about narwhals and those long, twisted horns that thrust forward from their heads?"

"Ice swords," said Ashevak. "That's what the narwhals have growing forward from their upper jaw. They always grow out of the left side and they always have a left-hand twist. Only the male narwhals show a horn."

"What do they use them for?" Matt asked.

"I think they use them to protect themselves," Ashevak answered, "and for punching thin holes through the soft slob ice so they can breath. If narwhals get caught for a long time underneath the ice without air, they'll drown just like any other animal or human."

"Did you ever see a narwhal thrusting its tusk up through soft ice?" asked Dr. Lunan.

"No, I never did," admitted Ashevak. "But some of our Inuit hunters say others have seen it happen long ago."

Dr. Lunan shook his head in disbelief, but he said not a word.

"Tell us other things you've heard," said Matthew.

"Many of the tales we know about narwhals," Ashevak said, "come from old times, far-off magical times, when the humans and the animals could easily talk together."

"Listen carefully. I can tell you something that may make Jill feel kind of scary," Kayak said. "I heard this from my grandmother."

"Tell us," Jill said.

"It's about a girl with beautiful black hair that she wove into two long braids. One hot day in summer, when the rocks beneath her feet were warmed by the sun, she took off her skin boots and pants and went wading in the water. Two sea gulls saw her, and laughing cruelly, they swooped down, each snatching the end of one of her hair braids. They flew around and around above her head until they twisted her braids into one long, stiff horn. Then, with one last hard tug, they tipped the girl over. She fell into deep water and began swimming, and she became Akalingwajuak, the mother of all narwhal.

"That's not all,' 'said Kayak. "My grandfather told me that on quiet summer evenings, if you listen, you can often hear those cruel gulls laughing and that same first narwhal swimming over the reefs with others, singing like birds through the blow-holes in their heads, making a sound so wonderful it sets the gulls to crying and all the sled dogs and wolves and foxes dancing and howling half the night."

"Do you believe that story?" Jill asked Kayak.

"Sure, I believe it." Kayak laughed. "Lots of strange things happened long ago when we all lived much closer to the animals and shared their ways."

Sandy Lunan smiled at them. "Southern biologists have no ancient tales about the northern whales, especially the narwhals. We will have to go down into the sea if we want to learn more about those strange, shy creatures. I would say narwhals are the least known and most mysterious mammals in all the oceans of the world. These days they are often called "sea unicorns." *Monodon Monoceros* is their Latin name. They are whitish in color and brown-spotted, almost like a leopard. Narwhals grow to about three times the length of a man, not counting that curiously hollow tusk that is packed full of nerves and is sometimes as much as eight or nine feet long. That ivory horn ends in a point that is always sharply polished, so they must use it for something.

"The waters around this island are known to be a place where narwhals have been seen in spring or summer. But nobody has lived on this island for a long, long time," said Dr. Lunan. "Let me show you what Ashevak found."

His flashlight cut through the foggy blackness as he led them to the rear wall of the supply tent. There, behind a high pile of boxes in the shaft of light, Matthew could see a bleached skull standing upright. The skull was as large as a ten-gallon drum. As Jill's father moved the light beam upward, they saw a long, twisted, ivory tusk. It was as thick as a man's wrist where it jutted from the skull, then tapered upward seven feet to a sharpened, swordlike point.

"That's the first sea-unicorn horn I've ever seen," said Matthew.

Jill ran her fingertips along the smooth ivory twist. "This is the first I've ever been allowed to touch. I saw one in the National Museum in Copenhagen."

"I've seen a few of them," said Kayak. "One trouble with them is when they get old, they dry out and break too easily."

Dr. Lunan, who was only of medium height, showed them this tusk was as tall as he could reach. "It belongs to Ashevak," he told them. "He says he saw it only because the wind had blown it free of snow. "It's such a good one, he should offer it to the Yellowknife Museum. Let's go back to the cook tent, and we can talk about it."

As she poured some cocoa, Jill asked Kayak, "Have your people known about narwhals for a long time?"

"*Ahaluna!* Certainly," he answered her. "We call them *agalingwak*. Inuit have been melting their fat into oil for our lamps and eating their *muktuk* forever. That's the thick, chewy layer of skin outside of their fat. You don't need to cook it. It's about the best food that anybody ever tasted. And their long, ivory horn is very useful when you can't find any wood to make harpoon shafts."

"At least a thousand years ago," Jill's father added, "early northern traders like the Vikings and Siberians were probably the first to bring those long, magical-looking spirals of ivory to the South. At first, they were believed by all to be the horn of a true land unicorn. At that time, they were so rare and precious that only royal families were allowed to possess them. In the Imperial Palace in Tokyo, at the entrance to the emperor's throne room, stand two very ancient narwhal horns. Centuries ago in Europe, two of them were traded for the equivalent of a million dollars.

"Sir Martin Frobisher was said to be the first English seaman to find the tusk of a dead narwhal on an Arctic shore during his voyage to Baffin Island in 1547. When he sailed back to England, Queen Elizabeth the First came down to Plymouth to greet him. They say Sir Martin bowed deeply and gave to his queen that rarest and most curious gift. 'Your Majesty,' he said, 'I know not whether this royal horn be from the unicorn of land or sea, but I do offer it to you with all my humblest gratitude.'

"Queen Elizabeth was delighted. She had the precious jewels. It was valued at forty thousand guineas, which the keeper of the royal purse reckoned would have been enough to support the queen's army fighting in the fields of Flanders for almost half a year."

"Why did she want her army to be fighting?" Kayak asked.

"I don't know exactly, but there was lots of fighting over land and piracy at sea in those early days," said Sandy Lunan.

"It is no good having people kill each other," said Kayak.

"Everything was different then," said Dr. Lunan. "Well, maybe not so different. A king or visiting noble-man would often be afraid to eat the food or drink the wine in his neighbor's castle, for fear of being poi-soned. Sometimes these noblemen would carry with them a cup made of a precious narwhal horn, which is always hollow. It was cut into pieces not longer than your hand, then each one was mounted like a drinking cup with a silver bottom and a golden han-dle. It was said that if poisonous wine was poured into such a cup, it would bubble and froth over as a warning to its owner.

"I can tell you another thing about a narwhal horn," Jill's father said. "Queen Elizabeth the First greatly admired the famous pirate, Francis Drake, and when she sent him out in the name of England to explore the Pacific and plunder Spanish ships in the New World, Good Queen Bess, as she was called, took her most precious unicorn horn down to Ply-mouth and lent it to her favorite admiral. Drake proudly had his armorer affix that rarest gift to the bowspirit of his ship, *The Golden Hind.* That was the voyage on which he and his crew were the first to sail around the world. It was widely believed in Eng-land that the magic of that royal unicorn horn had protected Sir Francis Drake and his crew on their long and dangerous voyage."

"I wonder if there are any more of those horns lying around the beaches of this island?" Matthew asked.

"I don't know," said Ashevak. "When I was a small

boy, my father brought me here in summer. At that time, no one lived here, and we found three *agaling-wak* tusks lying on the shores. We had no wood, so my father used the tusks to make harpoon shafts, just as Kayak said. He would gladly have traded the three of them for one straight piece of driftwood that would float."

"There are so many things we have to learn about the narwhal," Jill's father said. "Do the males use their long, thin tusks like marlin to stun fish that they chase up from the seaweed on the ocean floor? Do they use those curious sea swords in combat when they choose a mate? Why do the female narwhals not have tusks protruding from their upper jaw? Who protects their young? I hope we'll find out the answers to these questions soon.

"If the narwhals arrive here, Jill will dive, carrying a camera with color film in it. She's won quite a few prizes for her underwater photography. It's not enough just to see the actions of the narwhals and write about them. I need all the pictures I can get."

Wild, cold winds whipped across the waters for one whole week and prevented Matt and Kayak from making their first dive. But each day the sun grew stronger and daylight remained a little longer.

One morning, Matt looked out the cook-tent door and scanned the beach. The wind and sun had swept the pebbles free of snow. "Let's go for a walk," he said to Kayak.

When they were some distance from the tent, Matt

paused and kicked his way through one of the last snowdrifts.

"Mattoosie, are you looking for a unicorn horn?" Kayak said.

"I'd love to find one," Matt admitted.

"So would I," said Kayak. "I like living on this island," he added, as they walked along the icy shore.

Suddenly, Kayak squatted down and studied some small, smooth beach stones, He examined them with care. "This is one of them. I'm sure of that," said Kayak. "It's a lot better than an *agalingwak* horn."

"What is it?" Matt asked him.

"It's a lucky stone. They're so hard to find I've never seen one on the ground until right now. I've only seen lucky stones that are carried in some old man's hunting bag."

"How can you tell that it's a lucky stone?"

"Well, it's worn smooth," said Kayak, "and it's a bit flat, and it's shaped like a small lemming or a mouse. This end is its head."

"What are you going to do with it?" Matt asked.

"I'm going to take it back and paint two small, black eyes where they should be and a round, red mouth. A person who owns a lucky stone should leave food out for it to eat. They say each year a true lucky stone will eat and grow a little bigger and luckier as well."

"Stones won't grow," said Matt.

"Maybe not where you come from, Mattoosie. Maybe not in Vancouver or Ari-zoo-na, because I'll bet you never even tried to feed them there."

That evening, Matt received word from Foxe Five that his father and Charlie had flown south to Ottawa on a jet plane but would return in a few days.

May had turned into June and still the narwhals had not come. Matthew and Kayak squatted on their heels beside Ashevak, hunching themselves against the cold dampness of the Arctic morning. They stared out over the mysterious black water that remained open like a lake beyond the white ice that extended from the island's shore. Gray fog rose and drifted over the patches of sunlit waters that often seemed to boil with the powerful movements of the tide.

Matthew shuddered. "The way the air feels, I would never guess that June was here."

Jill's father, carrying binoculars, walked up behind them. "On the next good day, you two can dive with Jill. It's warm enough now."

Matthew turned to Jill's father. "I've got a question, Dr. Lunan. Are there any sharks up here?"

"Sharks?" said Sandy Lunan. "In the far north there's only one kind—that's a Greenland shark. It's true they're often huge in size, but they're not dangerous. They have skin tougher than the roughest sandpaper. The Vikings used their skins to smooth the hulls of fast sailing vessels. But don't waste your time worrying about Greenland sharks. They're bottom feeders. The cold water seems to numb their brain and makes them lazy. There are probably none around here, and there's no record of them ever attacking a diver."

"I saw a scary movie about great white sharks," said Matthew.

"Forget about sharks," said Kayak. "We both want to go down there. We want to learn more about seals and walrus and narwhals. Inuit know a lot about what sea beasts do above the water, but we don't know what they do when they go beneath. Some say seals got nice little igloos down there!"

Matt said, "Now you're talking make-believe."

"My grandfather said when he was a boy the world used to be flat, with four big, carved poles holding up the sky. "But since the white men came," Kayak continued, "there was a terrible storm and somehow the world got rolled up into a great round ball. My teacher agrees with my grandfather. She admits the world is round. Do you believe that?"

"Sure, I do," said Matt.

"Well, then, you're just like my grandfather. You must believe this world is full of magic."

The next day dawned clear, and flights of sea birds flew over to nest on Whale Island.

Kayak said to Matt, "I can feel it in my bones. Today is the day we are going to make our dive."

At breakfast, Jill asked, "Are you two ready to come down with me?"

"*Ahaluna*, sure, I'm ready to go," said Kayak.

"Me, too," said Matthew. "We're coming with you."

When they pulled on their wet suits over their long winter underwear, Jill asked Kayak, "Why are you looking so glum?"

"Because there is no pocket in this wet suit," he answered.

"Why do you need a pocket?" Matthew asked him.

"Where am I going to put my lucky stone?" Kayak said. "I don't like going down there without my lucky stone," and he showed it to them in his hand.

"My father or Ashevak will hold it for you," Jill said.

"It's not the same as having it down there," said Kayak, "but I guess that's the way it's got to be." He handed his lucky stone to Ashevak.

When they reached the ice edge, Dr. Lunan said, "Remember, only five minutes on this first dive. When I jerk your safety lines, all three of you come up immediately."

They stripped off their outer parkas and boots and, bending, slipped their feet into their diving fins. All three wet suits had close-fitting hoods.

"You think it's cold now," said Sandy Lunan, "but if you were diving in midwinter, you would have to wear dry suits, and they are lots more trouble."

"Wait, Jill! You're wearing your hair in braids," Kayak said. "Are you going to dive like that?"

"Sure I am," Jill told him. "It's the best way I know to keep my hair out of the way." She laughed and hid it from the sea gulls inside her rubber hood.

A gust of wind came whistling across the shore ice, rippling the water that lay before them.

"You'll feel cold when you first get in the water," Jill told them, "but later it turns warm. You'll see."

Each of them slipped a flat, yellow life vest over their heads and tied it round their waists.

"In an emergency," said Dr. Lunan, "pull on that life-vest cord to fire its gas cartridge. Your vest will fill with air and float you to the surface. The water here is only about thirty feet deep, so you can come up and won't have to worry about the change in pressure."

Ashevak handed them their lead-weighted belts, which they had tested in the saltwater of the tank to make sure the belt would let them swim up or down without much effort.

Jill's father gave her the "bang stick" the boys had seen when she was unpacking the day she arrived. It was thumb-thick and reached from her elbow to her fingertips.

"What's that for?" Kayak asked Dr. Lunan.

"There's a shotgun shell in it. You make it go off by poking it hard against a shark, if it comes too close. But sharks should never bother you in these cold waters," he said cheerfully. "You just might want to use it on a . . . well, on who knows what. A walrus might try to get too close to you, or perhaps a narwhal. We don't know anything about their temperament, and it's always best to be prepared."

"My fathers' always very cautious," Jill told them.

Ashevak strapped the air tanks onto their backs while Dr. Lunan checked that they had their breathing hoses and masks properly in place.

Matt felt very clumsy as his webbed fins flapped noisily on the sodden ice and his twin tanks bumped like a pair of frozen stones against his back. Kayak, walking beside him, slipped and almost fell. Cautiously, they made their way to the place where Jill was already sitting on the edge of the ice with her legs dangling in the water.

"When you go in," said Dr. Lunan, "heave off with both hands and turn sideways, so your tanks won't strike the ice. Watch Jill. She'll go first. You second, Kayak. Then Matt will follow. You can meet just beneath the surface, and Jill will lead you down. Breathe regularly. Don't worry about the bubbles you'll be making, and jerk on your line if you want to come up for any reason. There is no sound down there, so be sure to use hand signals to each other. Now off you go, and enjoy yourselves."

Kayak was delighted with the sight of Jill in her red diving suit treading water just beneath the surface, making friendly blinks through the glass pane of her mask. Suddenly, he saw Mattoosie come plunging down beside him. Briefly all three hung weightlessly underneath the water, sending up bright streams of air bubbles.

Jill pointed downward, and Kayak followed her, with Matthew swimming close behind him. Their lead belts made it easy to go down, so they felt the force of the tide only faintly. Slowly they kicked their fins, controlling their descent through the gray-green depths laced with soft, rippling webs of daylight from above. Now, for the first time they could see the mysterious ocean's floor rising up beneath them.

Matthew turned his head, and above him and to

one side he could see an almost endless field of ice. It was as though he hung at the entrance of some glacial cave. On the edge of the blue-white ice, moving against the light, he saw two dark shadows that would be Ashevak and Jill's father. The air he was breathing from his tanks felt very cold inside his lungs. Just for a moment, a wave of fear closed in around him.

Matt saw Jill turn and signal. Both he and Kayak kicked their flippers and held their arms close to their sides. In a moment, all three of them were swimming side by side, and all Matt's fears were gone.

Jill gave another signal, and they wheeled through the hanging curtain of faint light that was fading as they neared the sea floor. They leveled off and turned smoothly right, then left. Then Jill swam out ahead and led them once more in single file. Matthew was amazed to see that Kayak, in a short time, had become such a strong and confident swimmer.

As Kayak followed Jill, he wondered why he and Mattoosie had ever been afraid to dive. It was wonderful! He hoped they could do it every day. They passed a school of small fish that scarcely moved when the three divers drifted through them like a dream. Kayak turned and looked at Matt, who blinked his eyes and spread his arms like wings to show his surprise and pleasure.

For the first time, Kayak could see the stony bottom. Then, suddenly, out of the corner of his eye, he saw something moving below. It looked at first like a large, dark shadow hovering in the murky water.

Jill saw it, too. She gripped his arm and pointed upward. Matthew quickly followed both of them toward the surface.

They had scarcely started their ascent when they saw the mirror-smooth water above them begin to tremble and heave in a huge circle, as though it were being stirred by a giant eggbeater. Kayak could see sharp, silver waves rebounding off the ice. He looked at Matt in panic. Now the water was shattering like a huge pane of broken glass. Jill looked back at them and signaled, "Wait." They crouched just beneath the violently exploding surface, afraid to stay near the monstrous fish but too terrified to raise their heads above water.

IV

THE WHIRLING, CHOPPING MOTION ON THE SILVER SUR-
face of the sea kept spreading, growing worse. Now
Kayak could see a huge fish-shaped shadow hovering
above them, blocking out the light of day.

Jill signaled for them to follow her to a place at
the edge of the ice. Matt watched Jill cautiously poke
her head above the water, then he and Kayak did the
same. Ashevak jerked each of them out.

They heard a tremendous roar and felt an icy blast
of wind against their faces. Looking up, Matt saw the
helicopter. It was *Waltzing Matilda*, repainted bright
red-orange.

Kayak pulled away his mouthpiece and shouted,
"MMMattoosie, it's ggg-got to be Ch-Ch-Charlie. He's
ggg-got *MMMatilda* flying again." He could not
even hear himself above the roar of Matilda's spin-
ning blades.

The helicopter hovered, then leaned to one side. In the pilot's seat was Charlie waving at them. Next to him sat Matt's father, pointing down with a look of amazement on his face.

Kayak, Matthew, and Jill waved up at them. In answer, Charlie made *Matilda* circle around the way a dog does when it greets friends. The boys could see a crude drawing of a kangaroo that Charlie must have chalked on *Matilda's* side.

"He's a wonderful pilot," Matt told Jill, as the helicopter whirled away and landed on the ice, "even though he scared us half to ddd-death."

"Mattoosie, ddd-did you see that ter-ter-terrible drawing of a kan-gaaa-rooo? We've got to fix that sss-soon."

Matt's teeth were chattering so hard he could not answer.

"I was never underwater with a hel-hel-helicopter whirling overhead," Jill told them. "It scared me silly!"

Still shivering with cold, Matt and Jill and Kayak ran along the edge of the ice until they were close to the orange tent. Matt could feel deep cold piercing through his wet suit, making his spine tremble until he feared it would break loose from his ribs.

Ashevak took off their tanks. Jill's fingers inside her gloves were so numb that she could not even feel them. Jill's father and Ashevak had three padded thermal blankets ready to drape around them.

As his father and Charlie turned toward them, Jill said, "MMM-Matt, you look just like your father."

Matt said, "DD-Dad, this is Jill Lunan. I've nnnever been so cccold in all my life."

"Never mind the formal introductions until we get you three warmed up," said Dr. Lunan, as he helped Ashevak pull off their leaded belts and flippers. "Now, you three, jump inside the tent," he said. "We've got the kerosene stove going, and there's a thermos of hot chocolate in the shoulder bag."

"Oh, that feels good," said Kayak, as the three of them bent over, so their faces would catch the heat rising from the stove while their cold hands clutched the steaming mugs of cocoa.

Ross Morgan and Charlie were standing near the entrance when the three of them came out.

"It's good to see you, son." Mr. Morgan clasped Matt's hand. "We've been thinking about you and Kayak every day since you told us on the radio that you were out here watching for the whales. We didn't know you were scuba diving."

"It's great down there," Matt told his father. "It's a different world."

"How's the professor?" Kayak asked Charlie.

"Oh, he's fine now," the helicopter pilot said. "The doctors let him out of the Winnipeg hospital as soon as his niece arrived to fly with him to Germany. We saw him at the airport when we went through Montreal. He told us to say good-bye and thanks to both you boys. We had to tell him the bad news about our oil strike, but he only laughed and said he was glad we were all alive. Now we have to tell you what—"

"You can talk about all that when we get back to

camp," said Dr. Lunan. "I've only got three divers, and I want to keep their circulation flowing until they change into warm, dry clothes."

"I'll help with that," said Charlie. "If you two will take Ross back on one of your snowmobiles, I'll flip your three divers to camp in *Matilda*. She's hot as a kangaroo's pouch inside."

"This will be my first ride in a helicopter," Jill told him.

"Come on, I'll race you to her," Charlie yelled, and they all four dashed toward *Matilda* and flung themselves inside.

Charlie gunned the engine and his beloved waltzer rose into the cold, clear air, whirled across the snow-covered sea ice, and landed gently on a patch of gravel in the center of Dr. Lunan's research station.

Matt could see Uvilu and Susee looking from the entrance of the cook tent. They waved at them. Only when Charlie shut down *Matilda*'s engine did Uvilu step outside and call, "*Teatilarit?*"

"She's asking if we want some tea," said Kayak.

"Yes, please," called Jill. "We'll have some as soon as we change."

When Jill jerked open the cook tent's double plywood door, steam poured out. One by one they ducked quickly inside.

"It's good and warm in here," she said to Susee. "Maybe tomorrow you two would like to do the diving and I could stay home and cook." She laughed. "I love to cook."

Uvilu and Susee smiled and nodded agreeably,

though they did not understand a word Jill said. Their teeth shone snowy white and their cheeks beneath their dark spring tan were red as winter apples.

Uvilu put down her loonskin sewing bag. "Have you three been underneath the water?" she asked Kayak in Inuktitut.

"*Ahaluna!* Certainly!" he answered, feeling very proud. "It's silent and a beautiful blue-green down there. Only thing wrong," he added, "it gets a little cold and wrinkles up your face a bit. But I can learn a lot about seals and whales. I'm going to go again."

He held his chilled hands over the cookstove and felt his face begin to burn. Jill and Mattoosie joined him.

"Did you see anything down there?" Charlie asked them.

"Yes, I saw something moving near the bottom, and it was huge," said Kayak, "but I don't know what it was."

"I saw it, too," said Jill. "Maybe it was some kind of a big seal, or could it have been a walrus?" Jill asked Kayak. "It gave me a fright when I first saw it."

Matt told them, "I think it was only one of those big waving fronds of brown seaweed. They move as if they're alive."

"That was no seaweed," Kayak said. "It was something I never want to see again unless I have a long, sharp harpoon in my hands."

"Let's talk about something else," said Matt.

"Charlie, what did you mean when you spoke of bad news about the oil?"

At that moment, Matt's father came in through the small door, followed by Jill's father and Ashevak.

"Pull up a bench and have a cup of tea," Dr. Lunan said.

"You've got a good-sized, efficient-looking camp here." Ross Morgan spread his hands.

"That's because there were five of us at first," Jill's father said. "All divers. Just like the Olympics. One from Canada, one from France, one from Germany, one from Japan. You might say I was diving for the U.S.A. After I broke my arm, we decided it would be best to have the other four down at our 'D' station. That's about four hundred miles south of here, at Cape Dorset. They're completing our walrus study. I told them I would stay here with Ashevak and watch for narwhal until my arm's in shape for swimming."

"Don't rush it," Charlie said. "It looks as though you've got friends here and good, strong tents and enough to eat"—he pointed at the neat pile of food cases—"at least until we came and overcrowded your table."

"Glad to have you," Sandy Lunan said. "We've been kind of lonely on this island."

Matthew was almost falling off the end of the bench, trying to make room for his father, who looked at him again with a friendly twinkle in his eye. Charlie sat across the table with a wide smile on his face, proud that his *Matilda* was able to fly again. He had helped rescue her and had flown to the Foxe Five base where Mr. McKenzie had helped him spray her a beautiful flaming red.

After Ashevak's wife had passed them each a second mug of steaming tea and a bowl of thick, delicious caribou stew, Ross Morgan looked up at the white light of the kerosene pressure lantern and said, "This is a nice bright tent with a good-sized table. Would you mind if after dinner Charlie and I spread out our maps and studied the northwest coast of Baffin Island?"

"Use this camp as though it were your own," said Sandy Lunan. "There are five smaller tents here. The orange tent number 3 has got two extra cots, and you can throw down your kit and unroll your sleeping bags in there." As he spoke, he was flexing the fingers that protruded from his plaster cast.

"Nothing at all would be happening out here," he said to Ross Morgan, "if it wasn't for these three young otters. Jill gave Matt and Kayak two weeks of special training in our narwhal recovery tank. She's a certified instructor, and I checked them out as well. They have passed all the necessary tests."

"What a piece of luck," said Matt's father. "I've always wanted to learn to dive. These days I believe a good geologist with a sharp rock hammer would be wise if he went hunting minerals underneath the sea."

Charlie shook his head. "Did you hear that, friends? This bold man here wants to hunt all the gold and precious stones and minerals, not only in the highest mountains and the deepest valleys and the hottest deserts, but now he wants to stake his claims beneath the coldest waters of the world."

"You're right," Ross Morgan said. "If the two of us were younger, I'd start out by searching underneath the sea."

"Forget that!" said Charlie with a chuckle. "We're too old to learn to dive. You told me that we were going to turn into rich oil barons when we four made that strike on Prince Charles Island."

"And, believe me, we would have done just that," —Ross Morgan nodded—"if the government of Canada hadn't sold all those high Arctic oil leases to big oil companies a dozen years ago."

"So that's the bad news," Matt said, as he looked at Kayak. They had gone through so much finding that oil that it was hard to realize it wasn't to be theirs.

"That's the way our luck's been running lately," Charlie said. "We might as well look on the bright side."

Ross Morgan laughed. "Have you noticed how quickly this summer sun has melted almost all of the snow off the land? When we flew along the north coast of Baffin Island, it looked just right for a big find of hematite."

"What is hematite?" asked Jill.

"It's the richest kind of iron. You just wait," Ross Morgan said enthusiastically. "Charlie and I will bring you in some jet-black samples."

After lunch, the cold of the dive followed by hot food made Matthew's eyes droop with sleep. Lying back in his sleeping bag, he looked up at the red glow of the nylon tent. He tried, as he had a thousand times, to remember his mother's face, but just as his vision of her was coming back to him, he imagined the two cars crashing on the Arizona highway and then, in the thick smoke and fire- and police-car sirens, she disappeared. He settled back into an uneasy sleep and dreamed that he saw a huge white bear come stalking into camp. It stopped and stood eyeing him, its narrow head weaving from side to side, its blue tongue lolling out as it tried to decide whether it would rip open the thin-walled nylon tent used by Jill and her father or whether it would destroy the one in which he and Kayak slept.

Matt woke when he heard a heavy scratching on the outside of the tent.

"Get up," Jill called through the tent wall. "It's time to eat."

After dinner, Matt's father unrolled the aerial survey maps and spread them out across the table.

"See the colors on those maps?" Matt said to Jill. "My father can read and understand them all. Blue shows copper deposits, the dark red is iron. The green is probably silver and nickel. A map like that can be a big help to prospectors in the Arctic."

Ross Morgan rolled up the geological charts and replaced them in their metal cases. "Would one of you like to come along and share the luck with us?" Ross Morgan asked them.

"We're leaving early in the morning," Charlie said.

"No, no thanks," said Matt. "Ashevak thinks the narwhals will come very soon. I wouldn't want to miss them."

"I am crazy about flying in *Matilda*," Kayak said, "but I'm like Matt. I guess I'd rather stay and see the *agalingwak*. I want to hear them singing and watch them make the foxes dance."

"Well," Matt's father said, "maybe Jill would like to come along with us and see how flying prospectors work."

"Oh, thanks . . . I'd love to . . . sometime, Mr. Morgan. But we'll all three dive again, as soon as the whales come in."

"Yes, yes," Ross Morgan said. "I guess that's more exciting, but all of you be careful. Charlie and I have enough food rations, and we'll take those extra barrels of gas. We should be back here in a day or so, unless we're held up by bad weather." Matt's father clamped one of his huge football-player's hands on Charlie's shoulder. "We've spent our last penny to get *Matilda* in the air again. We're going to make a record find up here. You'll see."

"This feeling we have is nothing new," Charlie told Dr. Lunan. "It seems more natural for the two of us to be broke and hoping for good luck than owning our own oil wells."

Jill removed her down jacket. Under it she was wearing a faded blue shirt. The words across its front read NAVY DIVE CORPS.

"You certainly love that old shirt with the writing

on it," Kayak said to Jill. "When we get back to Frobisher, I'm going to buy you a bright new one at the Hudson's Bay Company."

Jill laughed shyly. "No, you're not. I've got enough shirts. I just wear this one because it's my favorite. My great-uncle was diving in the Amazon River in Brazil in this same shirt almost sixty years ago. Doesn't that seem wonderful to you?"

"What was your great-uncle diving for?"

"Emeralds and diamonds," said Jill. "But it was all very different then. Divers wore heavy bronze helmets, bulky canvas suits, and heavy leaded belts and boots. Great-Uncle Edward and a partner whose name was Jesus Ramona Del Gado. He was not a diver. But together they built a small raft. My great-uncle would dive down under the raft and walk along that enormous river bottom, searching for precious stones or any other kind of treasure. His partner's job was to pump air down to him through a rubber hose. It was a good idea they had, because no diver had ever walked the Amazon riverbed. They say those two found many diamonds.

"The only trouble was, when they got to a narrow branch of the river where white men rarely go, some Indians, who were the kind that wear only a few bird feathers and red orchids behind their ears, came out of the forest. One of those Indians aimed a nine-foot blowpipe at Jesus Romana Del Gado and blew a deadly poisonous dart into his side.

"That was the end of my uncle's partner, and, of

course, it was also the end of Great-Uncle Edward. Poor thing, walking down there on the river bottom, he must have wondered just what happened when the air pump stopped and his safety line went slack. He never got another gulp of air.

"This old faded shirt," said Jill, "is one of the only things the search party found belonging to Great-Uncle Edward."

"That sounds like an Inuit story," Kayak said. "But people in Frobisher only wear shirts for one year, maybe two, then they tear them into rags to clean rifles or pots. Do they do the same where you come from in Sandy-Aggoo?"

"Yes, that's what usually happens in San Diego. Old shirts just get thrown away or torn up into dustrags. But Uncle Edward's shirt is special. I wouldn't tear up his shirt for anything. It's probably the last one in the world."

Kayak laughed. "You're very proud of that shirt." He reached into his pocket and pulled out his old-fashioned folding knife with the bone handle. "This old trade knife is from the Hudson's Bay Company. It was given to me by my grandfather. I wouldn't give it away. It's the best thing that I own."

In the morning, Matthew waved at his father and Charlie, then stood with the others, watching, as *Matilda*'s blades whined into life with a steady *whirr, whirr, whirr. Matilda* rose above the camp, then disappeared in a silver blur of light. Charlie whirled the bright red waltzer round in a tight turn, then headed eastward from Whale Island across the flat, white ice toward the bare rock hills and the mysterious mountains of north Baffin Island.

When they went inside the eating tent, Jill began filling up their bowls with hot oatmeal porridge. "You two eat a good helping," she told Matt and Kayak, as she saw them sniffing the delicious scent of sizzling bacon. "Put hot butter and brown sugar on the porridge. That will help to keep you warm. My dad and Ashevak are getting ready to take us out for another dive. This time we may go underneath the ice. Do you think you're ready?"

Just hearing those words made it difficult for Matt to swallow his porridge.

At that moment, they heard Ashevak, outside the tent, begin to shout. "*Agalingwak! Agalingwagalook! Atouasik, muko, pingashut!*"

Dr. Lunan jumped up from the table. "What's he saying?" he asked Kayak.

"He's counting the narwhals. He has just seen one, two, three big narwhals rolling over the reef."

"Holy smoke!" said Matt. "They're here at last."

V

"HOW MANY NARWHALS DID YOU SEE?" SANDY LUNAN
shouted to Ashevak.

"*Tidlimut*, five!" Ashevak spread the fingers of his
right hand. "They were rolling over the reef, slap-
ping their tails, then blowing and chirping like a
flock of birds before they took in air and dove again."

"Nobody is to use the snowmobiles on the ice today," Jill's father warned them. "The noise could
frighten the narwhals. Like all the sea mammals,
they are said to have very sharp hearing, even when
they're underneath the ice. Put everything you'll
need into one rowboat," Dr. Lunan advised. "Then
Ashevak will lash it onto the sled. It will be easy for
the four of you to skid it over the shore ice to the
open water. Don't worry about me. I'll follow you,

but I can't really be of much help with this broken arm."

"You can sit in the boat on the sled," said Ashevak. "We'll give you a ride out there."

"No, no," Dr. Lunan answered, "the walk will do me good. But if they're ready to dive before I get there, I'm trusting you to keep a close watch over the three of them," he called to Ashevak. "And Jill," he said, "be sure that none of you stays down for more than ten to twelve minutes. Remember how cold you were yesterday? *Matilda's* not around to fly you home today."

Sandy Lunan hugged his daughter, then handed her his underwater camera. "If you're lucky enough to get a glimpse of narwhals, take lots and lots of pictures. But be careful," he warned. "Matt, you or Kayak be sure to take this bang stick down with you. No one knows what narwhals will do when they first see humans swimming near them in the water. Ashevak is going to hang a special microphone down into the water and, if it's turned right, we may hear narwhals calling to each other."

"Can you imagine that?" said Kayak.

They had not pushed the boat on the sled very far before Kayak stripped off his parka. Soon Jill and Matthew did the same. Like Ashevak, all of them wore dark glasses against the glare.

"These wet suits make you feel really warm," Jill gasped. "I never would have believed I'd feel so hot while walking on ice."

"Real summer's coming to us now," said Kayak.

"The geese are moulting. You should enjoy this fine gift of weather from Sila before she starts to whip up the winter storms again."

"Who's Sila?" Jill asked him.

"Oh, she's the big woman who controls the weather." He pointed at the sky. "My grandmother told us that Sila makes the sun shine or maybe she brings snow and fog and blizzards. There are lots of different spirits in the Arctic world."

"Well, Sila's making good weather for us today," said Jill.

"That's because she likes all of you," Ashevak told them, "and I think she's glad to see the narwhals back again."

"We're almost there," said Kayak. "Everybody stop talking now, and don't," he whispered, "say a word about the *agalingwak*, because narwhals can understand every word of Inuktitut and probably they know English just as well, and maybe even quite a bit of French. That's what some people here say."

"That's pretty hard to believe," Matthew whispered to Jill.

"He may be right," said Jill. "People who study sea mammals believe they are very intelligent. Whales seem to use sounds to communicate with each other, but even after years of study, we still can't understand their language. It's an important part of the narwhal mystery my father is trying to uncover. He wants to make underwater recordings of what the narwhals are saying to each other, then try to understand it with the help of advanced computers."

"I hope the narwhal will still be there when we go down," said Kayak. "I'd like to hear them talking underwater."

"I can't understand you," said Ashevak. "I like it right up here standing on the ice, or floating in a boat. That's seal and walrus country underneath the water, the wrong place for human beings."

Near the edge of the ice, they stopped and quietly unlashed the boat from the sled. In a few minutes Ashevak had the warming tent set up and was helping all three of them put on their air tanks and lead-weighted belts and life vests.

"Here," he said. "Tie on your safety lines. You must never go down without them."

Matthew looked out over the still water that shone like silver in the late-morning sun. Small ice pans drifted in the center of the open water, where flocks of sea birds whirred in and landed on the glass-smooth surface.

"Probably those narwhal are breathing through cracks in the ice," said Kayak.

"Well, let's go down and see," said Jill, as she wet the glass inside her face mask. She handed the bang stick to Kayak. "You're the hunter here," she said, "so I'll give you the gun."

"It doesn't look like a gun to me," said Kayak.

"Well, it is," said Jill. "If you jam it really hard against an animal or fish that attacks you, it will fire shot into it. But remember, be sure not to poke it hard at any one of us."

"I'll be careful," Kayak said. "All Inuit are taught safety when it comes to handling guns."

"I've never had to use one of those sticks," Jill told him. "I've never even seen one fired, although I've often been near small sharks and barracuda. I'm glad there're none of the dangerous types of sharks up here in these cold waters.

"Any questions?" Jill asked them, "because this is our last chance to speak or hear each other before we make our dive."

"How long will we stay down?" asked Matthew, looking at his wristwatch.

"Let's stay ten minutes," Jill said, "unless there's something terrific to be seen down there. Then we just might stay the full twelve before coming to the surface. Remember how freezing cold we were last time, and that was only five minutes."

They put on their masks and breathing regulators, then, sitting sideways, they heaved themselves off the ice into the cold blue water. Kayak looked up and saw that the strong tide had drifted him just beneath the ice. He judged it to be more than five feet thick. Against the undersurface of the ice he could see their air bubbles collecting, then spreading out in crowded patterns.

Together the three of them began thrusting downward, slowly kicking their fins, swimming like three brightly-colored fish among the gray-green shadows that rays of the Arctic sunlight were filtering through.

As they swam down through the icy waters, Matthew, for the first time, saw one of the two high stone reefs that Dr. Lunan had asked them to find. As they approached the first reef, Matt could see that it was made of granite and rose sharply out of the rusty-looking fronts of giant seaweed that moved smoothly with the ebb and flow of the tide. A large rock cod stared curiously at them, its front fins rippling like a pair of human hands .

Jill touched Matt's shoudler and pointed along the tumbled ridge of stone to where half a dozen large, white-bellied halibut moved slowly, like flying carpets, as they rose up from the reef.

Kayak's keen eyes saw something lying among the stones, and he swam down toward it. Picking it up, he found it was a beautifully twisted narwhal tusk, sharply pointed and golden ivory in color. The tusk was as long as he was.

Matt started looking along the reef, hoping he might find another tusk, until Jill touched his arm and the three swam on together.

Jill stopped and all three balanced upright, treading water with their fins and peering everywhere. They saw nothing but a pair of large, transparent stinging jellyfish. Looking down, they could see seaweed growing from the rocky bottom. Matt looked at his watch. More than four minutes had passed, and still no sign of whales. Jill eased the camera across her back and made a gesture with her hands that means in any language, "I see nothing."

Matt again looked at his watch. They had been down for six-and-a-half minutes, and he was already feeling the bitter cold. They started swimming slowly along the reef, when suddenly Kayak signaled to them. Jill and Matthew turned. Out of the pale-green distances, Matt could see first one, then two more large, blue-gray shapes coming straight toward them. These were not like the cod that had waved its tail sideways. These creatures propelled themselves by working their flat tails up and down.

As the strange shapes came nearer through the silent world of water, Matt could see that each had a long, slim ivory tusk. The three narwhals stopped, then began curiously circling the divers. It seemed to Matthew like a frightening fairy tale, having these mysterious sea unicorns so close to them. Kayak wondered if they were eyeing his new-found ivory harpoon.

Jill cautiously adjusted her father's camera and began following their movements. Using the strobe light, she took pictures as quickly as she could. The three narwhals continued to examine them boldly, sometimes from below and sometimes from above, where Matt could look up and see their pale-white bellies and the dangerous-looking lancelike tusks. The narwhals' backs and sides were rich brown in color and spotted like a leopard's.

As the narwhals drew in closer, Matthew shuddered inside his wet suit, partly from the cold and partly from a sense of fear. The air from his tanks had turned so cold it seemed to freeze his lungs. One quick rush, he thought, and those long ivory tusks could easily pierce straight through any one of us.

Matt looked at Kayak and the shark stick that dangled from his wrist. Between her mask and mouthpiece, Jill's face was blue and pinched with cold.

Jill turned and pointed with a nod of triumph. Behind the three big male narwhals came what Matthew judged to be a female. She was smaller than the males, with finer markings. And she had no tusk. Jill did a slow somersault of delight when she saw that the female had a baby narwhal clinging tightly to her back. It was blue-gray in color and about as long as Matthew's leg. It had no spots. Jill aimed her underwater camera at them, reset the focus, and continued taking pictures at close range.

Because of the cold, excitement, and some fear, Matt began shuddering so hard that he thought he would have to pull the safety line. He looked at his watch again. They had been down for eleven minutes and twenty seconds.

Without warning, a huge black-and-white torpedo form rushed past them, almost upturning all three divers. The male narwhals whirled around and pointed their sharpened tusks straight at this deadly-looking enemy, a full-grown killer whale.

Matt's shivering ended, as he saw the enormous high-finned sea beast stop, then try to dodge around the tusks, perhaps to get at the tuskless female and the young one. The male narwhals were too quick for the killer whale and again it faced three sharp sea swords.

Matt felt a quick tug on his emergency line. Ashevak must have seen the killer whale, for he was signaling the divers to rise.

Jill paused, then turned back for one last photograph of the narwhal's enemy. The killer whale seemed startled by her red suit and her sudden movement. It turned its attack away from the close-knit pod of narwhals and swam straight toward her. Jill kicked her fins and started rising fast toward the surface.

Matt watched in horror as the killer whale shot up after her, its high, black fin cutting swiftly through the ice-cold water. Kayak, swimming with all his strength, managed to get between Jill and the attacking killer whale. Looking no bigger than a toy soldier with the bang stick dangling from his wrist, Kayak pointed his new-found narwhal tusk at the huge open jaws of the killer whale.

VI

THE HUGE BLACK AND WHITE WHALE STOPPED AND hovered in the water not more than an arm's length in front of Kayak's outthrust ivory harpoon. Slowly it turned sideways to focus its right eye at the three strangely-suited divers who each let out long streams of silver bubbles. Then, in perfect imitation, it, too, let out three short streams of bubbles. The killer whale seemed puzzled. It did not rush at the curious creature that was pointing the long dangerous horn at it. These three were not seals that the killer whale could gobble down in a single bite. Cautiously it continued to follow the three aliens as they rose toward the white edge of the ice. It kept a safe distance between itself and the long, sharp horn that Kayak continued to point at its gaping jaws.

Jill's father and Ashevka watched in horror as the

killer whale swam upward after the three divers. As soon as each diver's head emerged, Ashevak reached out with his powerful arms and pulled the swimmer onto the safety of the ice.

Matthew looked down just in time to see the black-finned creature rise almost underneath their feet; then, with a violent slap of its broad tail, it splashed them all before it disappeared beneath the ice.

With his left hand, Dr. Lunan helped them unbuckle their oxygen tanks and take off the weighted belts and flippers.

"That was too close for me!" Matt bit his lip as he squatted trembling on the ice near Jill and Kayak.

"You were very brave," Jill said to Kayak, "putting yourself between me and that killer whale."

"It's really cold up here," said Kayak, shaking, as Ashevak wrapped blankets around them.

Matt said, "My lungs fffeel like they're fffreezing from sssucking in that ice-cccold oxygen."

All three of them crouched together, their shoulders touching, hunched like old men, their faces puckered blue, and their brains too cold to tell them quickly what to do.

Jill mumbled to her father, "We saw five narwhals."

"Hand me the camera, Jill. I'll thaw it slowly."

Shuddering still, they seemed afraid, at first, to talk about the killer whale. They spoke only of the hornless female narwhal and the young one that rode on its mother's back.

"I know I have some wonderful pictures of all the narwhals"—Jill shuddered—"and that killer whale.

Did you sss-see the way it swam in at the nnn-narwhals and then at us?"

"I'm glad that it didn't come any closer," Kayak said. "I wonder if it was afraid of this sea sword." He seemed surprised to see that he still clutched the narwhal horn in his left hand.

"Perhaps that killer whale *was* smart enough to be afraid of the narwhal spear that Kayak carried. But it was not afraid of you three," said Dr. Lunan. "No. It was simply curious. It was probably just coming up to study you in the same way we humans go down to study them. I believe you three have just been swimming around with some of God's most intelligent creatures. But never mind the talk. Start running for that warming tent."

When the three of them stood huddled over the small stove in the tent, Kayak unscrewed the lid from the big steel thermos bottle and poured each of them a tin mug full of steaming beef broth.

Jill said, "I kept praying Dad was right when he said northern killer whales have never been known to attack a human being."

"Maybe so," said Matthew, "but how often do killer whales get the chance to attack a human? Never! Unless they fall in the water without wet suits."

"Then they'll freeze dead—quick!" said Kayak.

"I read in school," said Jill, "that an Englishman named Shackleton used pack ponies on an expedition trying to reach the South Pole and that killer whales rose up and broke the ice around those ponies and ate most of them."

Matthew shook his head. "I feel sorry for those ponies."

"Me, too," said Kayak, "but it does prove that killer whales are smart."

Kayak jumped up when he heard the sound of running feet and pushed back the tent flap. Ashevak was running fast toward the sled behind his snowmobile. He snatched up his heavy rifle and knelt down on the ice, studying the water before him.

"He's seen something," Dr. Lunan said, "but I'm not sure what."

"*Tiaka, tiaka!* Look, look!" called Kayak, as the killer whale's high, black dorsal fin appeared and came knifing through the surface of the water.

Ashevak swung the rifle barrel until it pointed just below the plume of white steam that the killer whale blew upward from the twin holes in its head.

"Don't shoot!" cried Jill. "Don't shoot it!"

Ashevak turned and looked at her in amazement.

"That whale could easily have harmed us, but it decided not to. Why should we kill it?" she said.

The killer whale dove, then rose a second time, flashing the bold white markings on its cheeks and sides, before disappearing in a thick scattering of floating ice.

Ashevak jerked open the rifle bolt, and a heavy brass cartridge flipped into his hand. He laughed and shook his head.

"Maybe Jill is right," Matthew said to Kayak. "What good would it do us to kill it?"

"Killer whales are smart," said Kayak. "I'm sure they can easily tell the difference between fish and seals and human divers they have never seen before."

Jill's father said, "There'll be no more diving while that killer whale is blowing in this stretch of water. Ashevak will spend each day down here on the edge of the ice and keep a watch for killer whales. If they don't reappear for five or six days, then we might chance another dive." He held up his arm. "By that time, I'll have this fin of mine out of its sling. I swear I'm going to dive with you!"

That night, Kayak brought into the cook tent the narwhal tusk that he had found on the sea floor.

"Your lucky stone must be working—to pick up a wonderful thing like that," said Matthew.

"This ice sword is yours, Mattoosie," Kayak said, as he handed it to him.

"Oh, no. A thing like that belongs in a museum or in a castle with kings and queens."

"It belongs to you," said Kayak. "If you see a king walking around here, you can give it to him, if you want. But it's my gift to you. Keep it safe beneath your bed. That way we won't trip over it."

"*Nakoamiasit*, brother," Matthew said in Inuktitut. "That's the best thanks I can say."

Almost a week later, when they were having breakfast together, Kayak held up his hand and said, "Listen! That must be Charlie and your dad! I can tell the sound *Waltzing Matilda* makes even from far away."

Soon all the others could hear it—the distant *thunk-thunk-thunk* of a helicopter's whirling blades.

"I hope they've found gold," said Jill, "or even lead."

"I hope my dad's found something," said Matthew, as he drained his cup. "He and Charlie could use a little luck."

The red helicopter whirled around the tent, fanning the bright Arctic fireweed that grew all around until it flickered like flames. Charlie hovered for a moment, then landed *Waltzing Matilda* safely beside the summer stream on a wide, gray-green patch of caribou moss. Ross Morgan pushed open the door and climbed out one side, and Charlie jumped out the other.

"We didn't actually find anything," Matt's father told them, "but all the mineral signs are excellent. We're sure to find it next time."

Matt looked at his father and thought, poor Dad, why does it always have to be next time, then next time.

"Well," said Charlie, "your dad is always optimistic. Lets' just say we had a jolly good ride over some lovely open country and round, clear lakes. We saw walrus and caribou and half a dozen polar bears, but we didn't uncover a single ounce of pay dirt. I'm glad you're not asking us for rent on your tent."

"Charlie, did you bring our paintbox with you?" Matthew asked.

"Would I forget an important think like that?"
Charlie grinned.

"You might," said Kayak, "but you didn't. Now we
can put the kan-gaaa-rooo back on *Matilda*'s side."

"What are you two talking about?" Jill asked.

"You'll see," said Kayak. "Mattoosie does his part
and I do mine. We're going to start right now. Maybe
you can help us, if you like."

Standing by *Matilda*'s side, Kayak rubbed off most
of Charlie's crude chalk drawing of a kangaroo and
began anew. Matt thoughtfully mixed the paints.

"Kayak, you must have seen at least one kangaroo,"
said Jill.

"Never," said Kayak, as he carefully sketched the
outline. "But Mattoosie, he's seen plenty of kan-
gaaa-rooos in zoos."

Kayak carefully drew two young kangaroos in
Matilda's pouch. "Charlie told us they're called
'joeys,'" said Kayak. He paused, then drew in a
third small one.

"Who is he?" asked Jill.

"It's not a he, it's a she," said Kayak, and he smiled
at Matt. Finally he drew fins and a pair of oxygen
tanks on Matilda's back and small masks on all three
joeys.

"Now I'm finished," Kayak said. "It's Mattoosie's
turn. You watch him. He's going to paint on all the
color. He's really good at that."

"You two are quite a combination." Jill smiled.
"You can do almost anything together."

"That's right," said Matthew. "The two of us have

even got a private gold mine . . . but, well . . . we've kind of lost it for the moment."

"How can you lose a gold mine?" Jill asked them.

"Oh, that's easy," Kayak said. "This whole Arctic looks a lot different in summer than it does in winter. We found our gold in a river at the end of winter, then we lost the place in the summer. But that's where we first saw frozen fire."

While Kayak told Jill about the river where they had found the heavy golden nuggets, Matthew painted Matida.

"She's wearing fins instead of skis," Matthew explained to Jill, "because she's at this diving school. Jill, to bring all of us some luck, would you like to paint her back tanks blue?"

When they were finished, Uvilu and Susee came out and admired their work. Charlie beamed with pride.

Next morning after breakfast, Jill said to Matt and Kayak, "Let's borrow the big binoculars and go for a walk. We can take a picnic lunch. I want to see all of Whale Island now that the tundra is clear and birds are nesting. Anyone want to walk with us?" Jill called.

"You three go ahead," her father answered. "Ashevak and I are going to row out around the reef and see if we can see the narwhals through the window in the bottom of the boat."

"Thanks anyway," said Ross Morgan. "Charlie and I are going to study our geological maps and plan our next flight. Have a good time, but be sure to take a rifle with you. We flew over a pair of polar bears not far from here. They can be dangerous."

Together the three set out to explore Whale Island, which was still surrounded by a glaring field of heavy sea ice, now broken by a hundred blue lakes of melted snow.

"When the sun warms those shallow pools," said Kayak, "they will soon cut holes through the ice."

Almost all the snow had melted from the land except for long fingers of ice caught in deep ravines where the sun had failed to touch it. As they walked, screaming hordes of sea birds rose from their nests and wheeled along the island's eastern shore. They watched noisy Arctic gulls as they hovered high in the air dropping clamshells on the smooth granite rocks, then swooping down to see if the fall had smashed them open. If their first tries failed, they took the clams up higher and dropped them again.

"My dad says that's a bird using a tool," said Jill. "By dropping them, those birds are hammering the clams open on the rocks."

It was midday when they climbed the island's highest rock, which was smooth and sun-warmed. They lay down and rested.

"This is a perfect place, to eat our lunch," said Kayak. "We can look at Baffin Island with the bring-near glasses."

Matthew took the large ten-power binoculars out of their leather case and, steadying them on a rock, adjusted them for his eyes. "I'd like to go over to that part of Baffin Island," he said. "I'd like to see one or two of the lakes there that Charlie and my dad keep talking about. They say the ice has melted off them now."

"Nothing's stopping us," said Kayak. "Jill's father says we can borrow the other rowboat and its outboard motor and tow it behind the snowmobile."

"That's a rugged coastline," Matthew said, as he studied it with the powerful glasses. "Oh, now I can see White Tail Lake. Its entrance is a kind of reversible waterfall, according to Charlie. When the tide is out, the water pours down from the lake in feathery rapids. Later, when the tide rises, the seawater flows back into the lake. I'd like to go over there and watch from underwater, when its white tail changes."

"Spoken like a true diver," said Jill, as she borrowed the glasses. "That lake appears to be round, and, like a clockface, it has a strange dot right in the middle."

"It's too far away to be sure. Maybe it's only a rock," Jill told him.

"It's not a rock," said Kayak, who was peering at it carefully. "It's moving, and it's got a very strange shape."

As they hiked back to camp, the whole sky filled with copper-tinted wind-torn clouds and the wind moaned sadly as if it knew something bad was about to happen.

When the snowmobile came in dragging the boat, Kayak said, "I'm glad to see your dad and Ashevak home again. That ice should break up as soon as this wind starts working with the tide."

They helped Ashevak drag the boat high above the tide line and turn it over. Then they went and placed heavy rocks around the edges of all the tents and weighted down every other thing that might blow away.

"Look," said Jill. "Is that crack in the ice widening?"

"The tide is coming up. It's moving the ice," said Kayak.

Matthew turned around fast when he heard *Matilda*'s engine start to throb.

"Don't worry," said his father, who had come up behind them. "Charlie's going to move *Matilda* into that narrow gorge, where she'll have more protection from the wind tonight. Come and help us tie her down."

The sky turned dark purple, and near midnight a huge wind came with driving rains. So violent was the storm that Matt and Kayak got up and dressed. Each held one of the poles to keep the tent from going over. They held on until dawn, when the lashing wind passed over them and left behind an ominous silence.

Kayak untied the tent flap and stepped outside. "*Seekoo audluktok!* It's gone! All of the ice is gone," Kayak shouted, and he did a kind of dance. "Mattoosie," he said, "be glad for what you see there. It only happens once a year."

Matthew was too amazed to speak. Where there had been endless miles of solid, snow-covered ice,

there was nothing now but a vast sea of blue water
that sparkled as the morning sun broke through
shreds of racing clouds.

"Where did the ice go?" asked Matthew.

"Drifted far off to the southeast." Kayak pointed
at a faint line of white. "Some of that ice may come
back with winds and tide, but it won't stay long." He
clapped his hands. "Let's get Jill and show her what's
been happening while she slept."

Jill rubbed her eyes. "I can't believe it. I wondered
if the heavy ice would ever go away."

That day, the weather was bright and clear and
the water around Whale Island reflected the sky like
a giant mirror. Jill was excited by the trip they
planned to take.

"I'll get the food together," she told them, "if you
two will pack all our diving gear into the boat. Make
sure we have fresh oxygen tanks. My father says we
can use the outboard motor as long as we don't go
near the narwhal reefs."

The motor started easily on Kayak's second pull,
and he did the steering. "I wish I had a boat like
this," he shouted above the noise of the engine. "It's
really light and fast. That window in the bottom
hardly leaks at all."

After a half hour passed, Jill shaded her eyes. "I
can see the White Tail fall."

Kayak stood up cautiously to gauge the direction,
and he guided their speeding boat toward the plume
of white water that gushed from the lake into the sea.

By the time they arrived at the entrance to White Tail Lake, the tide had risen so high that the reversible fall had disappeared.

Kayak shut off the outboard engine. "Just wait," he said. "You'll soon see the tide forcing seawater into the lake."

A few minutes later, Matthew stood up cautiously in the wide-bottomed rowboat. "It's happening now," he said. "I can feel this boat being pulled by the tide."

"Sit down," Kayak warned, "and grab an oar for steering. We are going to get sucked through that little rock entrance very, very fast."

A moment later, the stubby boat seemed to shoot forward. It ran between two low, gray granite walls worn smooth by an endless ebb and flow of water. Matthew knelt in the bow, his long oar ready to fend off any rocks.

Suddenly they found themselves riding safely on the waters of White Tail Lake, whose surface was still partly hidden by morning mists. Once inside, they could see that the lake was round, with a stony shoreline. Beyond the narrow shore, the land was covered with a soft blanket of gray-green tundra, and this was dotted with countless thousands of blooming Arctic flowers.

"I don't know what it was," said Kayak, "but as we passed through, I saw something swimming just ahead of us."

"Maybe it was one of those red-bellied Arctic char," said Matthew hopefully, as he felt the side pocket of his pack for his hook and line.

Kayak turned his head and looked back at both of them. His eyes were wide. "Oh, this was a lot bigger than any char," said Kayak.

"How much bigger?" Matthew asked.

Kayak peered down into the water before answering. "This thing was maybe four times bigger than you are."

Matt felt a shiver run up his spine.

They drifted on the mirror surface of the lake. All three of them took turns staring down through the small window in the bottom of the boat. Sometimes they could see beds of brownish seaweed where great fronds waved lazily on the incoming tide. But they saw no living thing down there.

"Anything as big as that will have to rise to the surface to breathe air," said Kayak. "If we keep looking around us, we should see it."

They studied the smooth surface of the lake for a long time, but they saw no movement in the drifting mists.

"You must have been wrong," said Matthew. "Maybe you saw the reflection of a passing cloud."

"I thought of that," said Kayak, looking up, "but there's no cloud in the sky today."

"Let's forget it." Jill laughed. "Maybe you were seeing your own shadow."

"Will you pass me those bring-near glasses?" Kayak asked. "Maybe we can see what's out there in the middle of the lake."

He took one long glance, then hurriedly jammed the binoculars back inside their case. His face was serious. "It's no rock," he whispered. "It's some kind of a boat. Not an Inuit boat and not a white-man's boat, but something bad. I see more than one thing alive and crawling around out there."

"You're seeing things today," said Matthew.

Kayak passed the binoculars to him. "Look for yourself," he said.

They heard a distant tapping coming across the lake.

"I don't need to know who's making that sound or what's hiding in the water," Kayak said to Jill. "We should head back to the Whale Island camp as fast as this boat will go."

"I hate to run away from a good mystery like that," said Matthew.

"I'm just as curious as you are," whispered Jill. "Let's row over . . . just close enough to see."

Matilda

VII

JILL AND KAYAK AND MATTHEW LISTENED CAREFULLY.
Out in the mists at the very center of the lake they
could hear a steady *tap-tap-tap*. The two boys un-
clamped the outboard motor and laid it in the boat,
leaving room for Jill to take up the extra paddle and
steer. Then they began to row quietly toward the
unfamiliar sound.

Only when they had nearly reached the middle did
the boys hear Jill gasp. They stopped rowing and
looked forward.

"I can't believe my eyes," said Jill.

There before them in the thinning fog was the
strangest boat that any of them had ever seen. Its
lower part was made of walrus hide stretched over a
driftwood frame. Kayak explained that it was an
umiak, or woman's boat, and so cleverly did Inuit

95

women sew these boats that they were completely waterproof.

But this umiak was different from all others. Over its stern a crude skin tent had been erected. All around the edges of the boat hung many strangely different things. Six red reflectors and an old-fashioned lantern were tied beside half a dozen hand mirrors. As the boat rocked slowly in the water, the mirrors flashed, reflecting first the lake and then the sky. Aboard the boat all pounding sounds had ceased and any signs of life had disappeared. The only sound was the creaking of their oarlocks as Kayak and Matt rowed cautiously toward the curious boat.

Matthew stood up and reached to grab the bow. He called out, "Anybody home?"

First Matt saw a pair of strong, square hands that gripped the gunnels, then a shock of hair above a pair of staring eyes. Growling like a bear, the wild man shook his head at Matt in anger. The band of fox teeth he wore rattled like the snapping of a dozen little jaws.

Matt swiftly drew his hand away from the mysterious boat and Kayak backstroked with the oars until there was a safe distance between them.

"Get away! Keep off! Don't touch!" the wild man bellowed. "This is my boat. Do you hear me? Mine!"

The wild man's wife peeked out from behind the umiak's mast and, smiling, she waved her hand at them. "You stop that shouting," she called to her husband. "It's only those two friendly boys who came to see us before, when we lived in the ice cave, but this time they've brought a *Kaloona* girl with them, and, believe me, she's a tall one."

She had no sooner uttered those words than two dark-eyed children's heads popped up and stared at them.

"Friendly boys?" the wild man shouted. "Those two are awful! They're the very reason we've been forced to hide out here."

"Boys, don't you pay one speck of attention to him," the wild man's wife called out to them. "My husband always gets excited whenever humans come around. Tell me, who's that long girl you've got with you?"

"Her name is Jill Tudlik," Kayak said, giving Jill the Inuit name for loon, their translation of Lunan.

The wild man cackled like a lonely loon at night.

"You stop that," said his wife. "Tudlik's a lovely name. That girl looks nice and healthy. Would you like to bring her aboard and have some tea and plover's eggs with us? I would like our children to have a closer look at her."

"Yes, we would like to come aboard," said Kayak. "But first, would your husband mind shaking hands with the three of us?"

"Why should I shake hands with you?" the wild man shouted. "You're probably like most of the other whites. Next thing you'll be telling me is that they own this lake."

His wife hooted like an owl, then grinned at Kayak. "Don't pay too much heed to him, boys. You should have seen how wild he got last summer, when that red whirlybird of yours came roaring around our old bone house. I guess you were out searching to find my husband."

"Oh, no," said Kayak. "We were looking for the river of gold."

Jill sat wide-eyed, staring at the wild man, who was a sight to see. He was deeply tanned and had a wide, square jaw and cheekbones that stood out like goose eggs beneath his flashing eyes. He pointed straight at Jill, then once more made a crazy loon call in imitation of her name. The wild man had his sleeves pushed up for work, and Jill could see he wore a half dozen gold and silver watches from wrist to elbow on each arm. Most were broken, and the time hands had been thrown away.

"We won't come bothering you again," Kayak promised the wild man's wife. "Mattoosie's father and Charlie are far away, looking for treasures hidden in the ground, but Mattoosie and this girl, Jill, and I are not doing anything like that anymore." He pointed down into the water. "These days, we are swimming underneath the water, taking pictures of *agalingwak* with the long horn and other creatures living in the sea."

"Why are you doing a crazy thing like that?" the wild man roared at Kayak in their language.

"Her father"—Kayak pointed at Jill—"wants to learn much more about the narwhals. We are helping him."

"Why don't you tell him to live his own life and let the narwhals live in peace beneath the water?"

"What's he saying?" Jill asked Kayak.

"He's telling me he's mad at me," said Kayak, "for helping you whites to spread around and change the country. He's still mad at Mattoosie and me for driving him out of his hidden house of whalebone that he built underground. Later, when he tried living in a blue-ice cave, he says we drove him out of it, too. He says for some time he's been living here in the center of this lake, but now we've found him, so he's going to have to move again."

"Don't you three worry too much about him," said the wild man's wife. "He's just feeling grumpy this morning. Would you still like to come aboard and visit for a while? I'll see that he shakes hands with you."

"*Nakoamiasit*, thank you. We would all like that," said Kayak.

They drew their rowboat up beside the curious-looking skin craft, and the wild man shook hands hard as he helped each one aboard. Jill brought with her some hardtack biscuits, a tin of corned beef, and a jar of honey. She passed the food around to everyone.

The two children were dressed in sealskin clothing. They were shy at first, but soon they were both sitting on Jill's lap. To the small girl she gave the key from the corned-beef tin to wear around her neck.

"This tastes good," said the wild man's wife. "Makes me wish I was living back in Frobisher again near that Hudson's Bay store where—"

"Silence, woman!" the wild man roared. "We've

got the only good things from civilization right here on this boat. All stuff the Air Forces threw away." He pointed to the cracked shaving mirrors on the mast and the rusted, red truck reflectors that he had hung around the edges of the umiak. "I guess our boat tent looks kind of strange, but it keeps the sun and rain off me while I'm working."

He took the last bite of his biscuit and pulled away a child's yellow-plastic raincoat. Hidden beneath it stood a partly finished carving of a walrus. The wild man took up his strangely shaped hand axe and started thoughtfully chipping at his work.

"That's going to be a wonderful-looking carving," Matthew said. "Where did you get such a large piece of yellow stone?"

"Its' not stone, stupid. It's *tugak*. Ivory," the wild man growled.

"That can't be ivory!" Kayak snorted. "No walrus has a tusk as thick as that."

"I didn't say it was walrus ivory," the wild man said with a chuckle. "It's ivory from some other kind of a great tusked beast that fell down and died a long, long time ago. We found it over there in the shallow water of the lake."

"It's true," his wife agreed. "Me and the little ones had to help him pull that big tooth out. When we stood it up on end," she said, "its curved point reached high above our heads, and it was as thick around as the fat part of my leg. That's how big it was."

"It weren't no one-tusk narwhal, so I suspect its

other tooth is lying somewhere over there." The wild
man stopped with his small axe in midair. "I didn't
need the other one. I don't aim to sell these carvings."
He pulled away a sealskin to uncover three others.
"No. I'm just going to leave them standing one on
each of the four sides of this lake. Over there to the
north, I'll set this carving of a human staring up at
the stars. Over there to the south," he pointed, "I'll
put this fish spirit to guard the lake. To the east, I'll
place this bird to sing at sunrise. Now, this last one,"
he pointed to the nearly-finished walrus, "when I've
got it polished, is going to stand over there in the
west, watching the entrance to the lake. When this
one's done, we will move away from here. Do you
know any nice lonely places where we could go and
hide?"

"We met some Tunik hunters not so long ago,"
said Kayak.

"Which direction were they going?"

"North," said Kayak, "and inland with the caribou."

Jill asked Kayak, "Why would he want to move
away?"

"Because, he says, we're chasing him and he feels
crowded," Kayak explained.

"Oh, it's not only you," the wild man shouted to
Kayak. "There's some strange thing swimming around
this lake at night. We hear it rising, splashing. Then
there's that noisy whirlybird flying around this lake.
It's enough to drive a decent family crazy."

"He's probably right," said Matthew, as they

climbed back in their boat. "Let's not disturb him anymore."

Kayak, when he set the oars into the locks, said, "Do you mind if we look over the place where you found that tusk to see if we can find the other one?"

"*Ataii*, go ahead! Look all you like," the wild man said, and he pointed the direction. "You can't hurt the animal that wore this tusk because she's been dead for years and years and years."

"How do you know it was a she?" Kayak asked him.

"Because a male tusk wouldn't have the kind of long, thin, delicate curve that this one's got."

The wild man's wife blinked her eyes at Jill and began to cackle like a hen. "You three can come back here and have some nice goose eggs with me after you're done digging. Try to forget all the awful things my husband has to say."

The wild man did not even hear her words, for he was already squinting at his walrus carving and planning the shape it would take. When he found the answer, he began to sing and chip away at the ancient ivory.

Jill steered while Kayak and Matthew rowed toward the lakeshore.

"When I was living down in San Diego," Jill whispered, "I never dreamed that I would ever meet a family anything like that."

"We know how you feel," said Matthew. "Kayak and I used to think that wild man was completely crazy, but now we've met him three times, and . . . we're not so sure."

They rowed in silence, listening to the fading sound of the carving axe.

"That must be the place," Jill said, as she pointed to a curve in the shore where a stream flowed into the lake. "You can see their footprints in the silt and the hole where they dug out the tusk."

After landing, the three searched everywhere, but they could not find the other tusk.

"I'm going behind those rocks to put my wet suit on," said Jill. "You two can do the same somewhere. I think we'll have to dive, if we want to find that other ivory."

As she got back in the boat, she said, "Let's try rowing straight out from here. The lake water is clear enough, and we may be able to see the other tusk. It should be lying on the bottom."

Jill knelt in the boat and shaded her eyes as she looked down through the viewing window. Slowly Matt rowed outward, and Kayak sat in the stern and steered.

"See anything?" he asked.

"Nothing," answered Jill. "Maybe we should turn around and go back toward the shore."

As Matt was pulling on his right oar, changing the boat's course, Jill said, "Wait! Hold steady. Don't move. I see something like a curved branch of wood down there. Lower the anchor and measure how much rope we let out. Then we'll know how deep it is beneath us."

"Only fifteen or sixteen feet," said Matthew.

"I won't need a tank for that," said Jill. "I just want

to go down and see if that really is a tusk. Give me one end of that nylon rope and tie the other end to the boat."

Almost before Matt and Kayak knew what she was doing, they saw her slip off her parka. Her red suit flashed as she dove smoothly into the water. Kayak and Matthew watched her go.

"She's a wonderful swimmer," Matt said. "Some girls would be afraid to go down there alone. But not Jill. She's brave."

"I like her a lot," said Kayak. "If I didn't have a wife already spoken for since I was two years old, I would ask my dad to ask her dad to let me marry her."

Matt, who knew much of Inuit ways, was not surprised. "I really like her, too," he said.

Jill had been under for less than half a minute when her head popped to the surface again. "I was right," she gasped, and taking a deep breath, she dove again. When she came up this time, she said, "I hope my seaman's knot is strong enough to hold it. You two try pulling the rope."

Kayak and Matt each took a grip on the rope and pulled upward, but nothing happened.

"You probably tied it to a heavy rock," said Kayak.

"No, no." Jill laughed. "You try again."

This time they could feel the weight ease slightly.

"Hold on," said Jill. "I'll get in the boat and help you."

All three of them pulled hard together. Slowly, hand-over-hand, they were able to bring up their heavy burden. The point of the huge tusk rose out of the water, dripping like a dark-brown serpent's tail.

"Holy smoke!" said Matthew. "We found it!"

"And there're others down there," Jill gasped, "not just two or three. I saw a dozen of them."

Together they struggled until they were able to tip the long tusk inboard. It was almost the length of their boat.

"What are we going to do now?" Jill asked.

Matt glanced at his wrist watch. It was 4:37 P.M.

Kayak held up his hand. "Listen. Can you hear the reversible falls?"

"No," said Jill.

"That means the tide's still high," said Kayak. "We could row out now, and, using the engine, we should get back to Whale Island in time for dinner."

"Good," said Matthew. "I'm starving, and I can't wait to see Jill's father's face when he sees this tusk. But before we leave, we must set up markers so we'll be able to find this spot again."

They piled two stone markers on the shore. Then, with Jill steering and the two boys rowing, they did not have far to go before they slipped through the narrows and out to sea. There was no wind and no ice in sight along the coast. They clamped the outboard motor onto the stern and went speeding west toward Whale Island, proud of their great, curved ivory treasure.

"What have you got there?" asked Ashevak, who had come down to help them at the smooth rock landing. "Is it *kayuk?*" he asked, using the Inuit word for wood. He knew that no trees grow on Baffin Island, but sometimes driftwood gets caught in the ice and tide and comes drifting from the northern coasts of Russia.

"It's not wood," said Kayak. "It's some kind of ivory tusk."

"No walrus ever had a tusk that big," said Ashevak.

"We think it's some kind of gigantic elephant's tusk," said Jill.

"We got no elee-phaants," said Ashevak. "We never had the elee-phants."

"Maybe you used to have them around here," said Matthew, "thousands and thousands of years ago."

"I never heard that in the old stories," Ashevak said, and Kayak agreed with him.

They dragged the boat and all their gear high up on the shore. Then Ashevak and Matt and Kayak went back and heaved the heavy tusk onto their shoulders. Jill held the tip, trying to share as much of the burden as she could. The four of them walked past *Matilda*, who seemed to squat on the tundra watching them, her long propeller blades drooping in the clouded evening light.

Two lanterns were glowing through the red nylon of the cook tent, as Matt opened the entrance, and together they marched their curious treasure in and eased it down until it leaned full-length against the table.

"What have you got there?" Ross Morgan asked them.

"It can't be what I think it is," said Dr. Lunan.

"It is," said Charlie, as he ran his hand along the cold, smooth surface. "I swear it's some kind of a great ruddy oversized elephant's tusk. I used to fly the ordinary ones from Burma to Hong Kong."

Dr. Lunan put on his reading glasses and examined the ivory carefully. "Charlie, you're right," he said. "It's a mammoth tusk. These three must have found it in a lake."

"You're right, Dad," said Jill. "How did you know that?"

"If it had been exposed on the ground, it would have rotted, and if it had been in the sea, the grinding ice and tides would have carried it away. But these cold, still Arctic lakes can be treasure-houses. This enormous ivory tusk," he said, stroking it with reverence, "has come off a hairy mammoth. That beast could withstand the Arctic cold, but my guess is that it may have fallen through the ice."

"There was a stream nearby," said Kayak, "that would have weakened the ice."

Jill looked at Kayak and at Matt. "There are a lot more tusks where this one came from. They were scattered in the lake."

"Did you mark the spot?" said Charlie. "I hope you staked your claim the way we do."

"Well, we sort of staked it," Matthew said. "We've got two stone markers set up on the shore."

"Sounds good enough to me," said Charlie. "A load of ancient ivory like that is probably worth a fortune. You've got no idea how much a wealthy Chinese merchant would be willing to pay for this one tusk. In Hong Kong or Taipai, my guess is, he might offer you as much as fifteen or twenty thousand dollars."

"Twenty thousand dollars!" Jill held her hands against her cheeks. "If that's true, then the wild man helped us all to find our fortune."

Charlie shouted, "We are grateful to the wild man, yes, we are, yes, we are. You show me the place and *Matilda* will do the heavy work." Charlie began to dance then sang:

> "Up jumped the jolly swagman
> And he dashed into the billybong
> We'll go awaltzing Matilda with you,
> Waltzing Matilda,
> We'll go awaltzing Matilda with you."

He clapped his hands together. "This lovely ivory will pay for all the repairs to poor old *Matilda* and let us go on prospecting."

"Better not count on that," said Matthew's father. "I was reading the export rules for the Northwest Territories, and you can't send raw ivory out of this country unless the Inuit have carved it."

"That's a good rule," said Kayak. "Finding old ivory is going to be wonderful for the carvers."

"You're right," said Matthew. "Finding mammoth tusks is something good that we could do for them."

"Righto!" said Charlie, catching his breath. "In the morning, if the weather's fair, Ross Morgan and I will leave early with *Matilda* to go prospecting. If we see you three over at White Tail Lake tomorrow, we'll drop in and pay a visit. If you've found some other tusks, Matilda will be glad to help lift out the ivory."

After breakfast the next day, they headed off in three directions. Jill's father, with his fifty-power telescope, and Ashevak went in one rowboat to keep watch over the narwhal reefs. Mr. Morgan and Charlie left to examine the north Baffin hills for signs of metal. Matt, Jill, and Kayak took the other boat and headed for the coast.

Using the outboard motor, they arrived just in time to take advantage of the high tide, which carried them swiftly through the narrows into White Tail Lake. The first thing they saw perched on a high stone was the wild man's walrus carving. In the midsummer sunlight, the ancient ivory seemed to glow with life.

"There it is. That means he's gone," said Kayak. "Too bad we had to crowd him out of here. I hope he find the Tunik people."

"I'm sorry, too," said Jill. "I'm worried about his wife and children. Where will they go now?"

The day, which had dawned clear blue, had started to cloud over by the time they rowed to the place where they had set up the two stone markers. They dropped their anchor.

"You dove down yesterday," Kayak said to Jill. "So today, why don't you stay up, and Mattoosie and I will go down together. We really want to see those tusks."

"Well, I guess that's only fair," said Jill. A look of worry crossed her face. "You two be careful." She helped them adjust their oxygen tanks and watched them put on their fins and face masks. She attached a safety line to each of them, then loaded and handed the bang stick to Matt.

This time Matt was to be first into the water. But he did not know how to enter from a small boat. Jill taught them both how to sit on the edge, facing inboard, then somersault backwards into the water.

"Leave your lead belts. You won't need much weight. You'll see it's different here. The water is half fresh, so you won't float as easily as you do in saltwater. The time is 1:28," Jill said. "Check?"

Matt looked at his wristwatch and said, "Check!"

"On this dive, I think you should stay down not longer than seven minutes. I'll see you at 1:35. Come up and tell me what you've seen. Check?"

"Check."

They both waved at her as they went under, each carrying his tight coil of safety rope.

The water did feel different. It seemed clearer, even though there was no bright sunlight shining above them.

Matt led the way, since Jill had handed him the bang stick. No killer whale down here, he thought with pleasure, as they swam down through the crystal-clear water of the lake. He could easily see the bottom. The only unusual thing was the abundance of fish. Schools of Arctic char floated before them, moving like transparent ghosts in the pale-

green water. They, like the rock cod, seemed not at
all afraid of the divers.

Matt saw Kayak look at his wristwatch. It was 1:33.
Perhaps they had anchored in the wrong place. Then,
on the lake's floor, Matt saw a mound of gray stone
boulders and curiosity drew him to it. Feeling like
a pair of mountain climbers, they swam easily across
the mound of stones. On the other side, they stopped
and stared in wonder. There below lay a great scattering of dark-brown ivory mammoth tusks. Together
they swam down and ran their hands along the
ancient elephant ivories. Most of them were strangely
curved and larger than the one Jill had found the
day before.

When Matt felt a sharp tug on his safety line, he
looked at his watch. Yes, Jill was right. Their seven
minutes were up. He swam to the nearest tusk and,
treading water with his fins, tied the end of his rope
to it with a granny knot. Then he slowly began
propelling himself toward the surface.

Kayak had waited a moment longer while he
double-tied his line to one of the tusks. Matthew
looked back toward Kayak, and as he did, out of the
corner of his eye, he saw a dark shadow rising,
slithering around the mound of rocks. It did not wave
its tail up and down like a narwhal or the killer whale
that they had seen. Its tail moved sideways. It was
a fish of monstrous size. The creature was four times
longer than Kayak. Its belly was deadly pale, and it
had a sharp fin on its back.

Matt's mind went racing back over all the pictures he had seen in Dr. Lunan's book of whales and fishes. Yes, he was sure of it. This terrifying fish that he saw coming up behind Kayak was an enormous Greenland shark. Its mouth was gaping open.

VIII

MATT WATCHED IN SILENT HORROR AS THE HUGE SHARK
rose through the icy waters, swimming toward
Kayak's dangling legs. Kayak was looking up toward
the boat and did not see the shark coming after him.
At that moment, Matt remembered that he, not
Kayak, held the bang stick in his hand. He dove down
through the cold green water, trying desperately to
reach his friend.

Kayak must have felt a movement in the water,
for he turned, and as he did, the huge shark grazed
him in the ribs with the hard point of its snout.
Then, propelled by the driving movement of its tail,
it spun Kayak over and over against the full length
of its body, rolling him like a broken puppet against
its rough, spotted flank.

Before Matt could reach it with the bang stick, the

huge shark swam away. Matt turned back and caught Kayak in his arms. Kayak's wet suit had been torn wide open by the rough skin of the shark, and a dark swirl of blood came from his neck and side, leaving a red cloud in the water. Matt shook Kayak, trying desperately to revive him, for he could see that no bubbles rose from his regulator.

Looking behind himself in terror, Matt wondered if the shark would come back. He jerked three times hard on Kayak's safety line, and then his own. Kicking his finned feet frantically, he tried to carry Kayak upward, using all the strength that he possessed.

Terror gripped him when he saw the huge shark coming back at them. This time it lashed its tail excitedly at the sight of Kayak's blood, which hung like red ink in the water.

Matt held the bang stick out toward the shark, when suddenly the lake's surface up above his head seemed to smash like a huge glass window. Jill had seen the shark and without her tanks had dived out of the boat to help him rescue Kayak. Once she got on the other side of Kayak, they swam hard together, towing him toward the surface. Matt could almost feel the huge shark crowding close behind them.

When their heads shot up above the water, they were not more than an arm's length from the boat. Between them, they dragged Kayak to its side. His bloody head hung sideways, and his wet suit was torn wide open. Jill steadied Kayak with one hand as she helped Matt pull Kayak's mouthpiece away, take off his heavy tanks, and let them sink toward the shark. Then together, with one powerful thrust, they raised Kayak and tumbled him halfway into the boat. Matt quickly hauled himself around to the other side and acted as a counterweight. Jill clambered in and pulled Kayak's legs to safety.

"It's coming again. Get out of that water quick!" she screamed at Matt, as she peered down beneath him.

She gripped both his wrists. Fear gave Matt super strength, and he shot out of the water into the boat.

All three of them lay gasping and shuddering from cold and fright, as gusts of icy wind swept across the lake. Jill and Matt listened to Kayak's heavy breathing.

When Matthew caught his breath enough to speak, he said to Jill, "I read in your dad's book . . . that Greenland sharks . . . were not supposed to hurt you! Just look . . . what that big brute . . . did to Kayak."

Jill knelt beside Kayak. "That shark didn't bite," she said, "it just rubbed up against him. Greenland sharks have skin that's rougher than the roughest sandpaper. Its skin tore Kayak's wet suit from one arm and his chest and shoulder and scraped him terribly across his face. If we don't get him bandaged soon, I'm afraid he'll bleed to death."

"We've got no bandages," said Matt. "Your dad's first-aid kit is back on Whale Island."

"You help me out of my suit," said Jill, and she held her arms toward him. "Now turn your head away. I'm going to strip," she said, and she pulled off her great-uncle's Navy diving shirt.

"Matt, I guess you'll have to turn around now because you've got to help me hold this. I think Kayak is coming to. He's moaning."

When Matt turned back, he saw that Jill was stripped to the waist and was busy tearing her lucky shirt into long, narrow bandages. She was shaking with the cold.

"Just hold this end while I bind the bandages around his head and neck. Be careful," she warned. "Don't cover up his mouth or nose."

When she said that, Matt saw one of Kayak's eyes open slowly between two layers of her torn cotton shirt. His lips were blue with cold, and his teeth were chattering.

"J-J-Jill, you get-t-t-t some clothes on," Kayak moaned, "or you'll freeze d-d-d-dead in this bad wind."

When Jill had Kayak's bandages tied, Matt pulled down his own wet suit and tugged his thin wool sweater over his head. "You put this on right now," said Matt.

"What about you?" asked Jill. She was hugging herself for warmth, but she was trembling from head to foot.

Matt pulled his sweater over her head and when she had it on he helped her pull up her wet suit. By this time his own green rubber suit was covered inside with white hoar frost, and when he put it on again, it felt like slippery ice against his naked skin.

They both scrambled into their summer parka shells, wishing they had their heavy winter wear.

Matt looked at the white waves that the rising wind was whipping across the lake. "Without Kayak's help, I wouldn't want to cross that rough stretch of open sea between here and Whale Island."

They jammed both sets of oars into their locks and began to stroke hard.

"Holy smoke!" Matt exclaimed. "The two tusks are still tied to the thwarts."

"Cut the lines," said Jill. "We've got to get Kayak in to shore."

Matt reached in his knapsack, drew out his knife and slashed the two lines free.

"Hurry, start rowing," Jill said. "The bottom of this boat is freezing cold. Kayak is shuddering. He'll die if we don't get him to some warmer place."

They rowed to shore as quickly as they could. Each took a firm hold on Kayak and eased him out of the boat.

"Where are we going?" Kayak gasped.

"For a walk," said Jill. "We're going to take you up to that dry moss where the tundra looks soft as any bed."

"Sorry, can't do it," Kayak mumbled, as they tried to stand him upright. His legs kept bending like a rubber doll's.

"You've got to try and walk up there with us," said Matt. "It will help you warm yourself. We've got no tent, no stove out here."

By putting his arms around their necks, they half

carried Kayak to Jill's chosen resting place and laid him down. Matt looked at the waterproof black watch strapped to his wrist. The time was 4:14. He glanced at Jill, who now crouched beside Kayak, trying to protect him from the freezing wind. When Matt stood up on tiptoe, he could see Whale Island in the distance. But even as he stared, thick fog came rolling in to hide it. The low stone hills around them and soon the whole lake disappeared.

When Matt looked at Kayak, all he could see was a narrow eye slit and a mouth slit in the bandage. The bandage read in faint blue letters, NAVY DIVING C. Blood was seeping through in an ever-widening patch. Jill's lips were still blue, but some color was starting back into her face after their rowing.

Matthew listened carefully, hoping he might hear the sound of an outboard motor or a helicopter, but there was only the moaning wind.

"Somehow we've got to get him to a hospital," Jill whispered, "or at least a doctor."

"Why didn't we bring that little tent," said Matt, "and some medical supplies?"

Near the entrance to the fog-hung lake, they heard a violent splash.

Matt cupped his hands around his mouth and shouted, "Who's there? Please help us!"

The echo of his voice came back to them, crying, "Please help us, help us, help us." Matthew could hear a loon laughing—or was it crying?—out in the drifting fog. "I guess it was the shark," Jill said, "going out to sea again."

"Oh," said Matthew. "I wish you hadn't told me that."

From beneath the boat, Kayak spoke weakly, but clearly. "Mattoosie, if a bear comes near us, you and Jill start barking like a lot of dogs. My grandfather said sometimes that helps drive a bear away."

"He must be feeling better, if he's making jokes with us," Matt said to Jill.

Jill reached in and felt Kayak's forehead. "No, he's not joking," she whispered. "He's just trying to cheer us up. I think he's running a high temperature, and right now there's nothing more we can do to help him."

They took turns trying to sleep until dawn finally came, and with it, a bone-numbing morning cold. The rising wind came off the sea, driving in more fog.

"What's that sound?" said Matthew. "Listen!"

Out of the north, they both heard the heavy *thunk-thunk-thunk* of *Matilda*'s whirling blades.

Matt leaped to his feet and raced up the hill. He reached the highest stone just in time to see *Matilda* pass like a gray ghost not far to his left. Then she went out of sight. But they could hear her churning in a great, low circle around the lake. Matt tried desperately to see through the fog. Then the sound of the helicopter faded as she headed west, probably to land on Whale Island.

"They're gone," said Matt, when he got back to their fires. "The fog's getting worse and our rowboat wouldn't stay afloat one minute in that pounding sea."

"We must make some kind of shelter for Kayak," Matt said.

"But we've got nothing," said Jill.

"The boat," Kayak whispered. "Use it like a house."

"He's right," said Matthew. "Come and help me drag it close to him."

Most of their feelings of cold had gone by the time they had skidded the boat to where they wanted it. Jill knelt down and felt the ground. "This wind has dried the tundra. But hurry! This fog will soak it wet again."

Together they carefully rolled the boat over until it covered Kayak, then they propped it up on the off-wind side with a pair of skull-shaped stones. Jill reached in and tucked the small canvas tarpaulin that was used to cover the engine around Kayak's body.

"I guess we can't have a fire," said Jill. "There's not a scrap of wood in this whole country."

"Burn the tundra," Kayak said with a groan. "Roll it up and light it now, before it gets too wet."

Matt could dig up the tundra easily. Using his fingers and his Swiss Army knife, he rolled it like a doormat. He felt around in the pockets of his thin nylon parka until he found the tube of emergency matches. Shielding a match from the wind, he struck it and was surprised at how easily the dry moss burned. It gave off a thick, white smoke, a rich, sharp smell. Kayak sighed with relief when he felt the welcome heat.

Matt and Jill built not one but two fires, just as close to the opening beneath the boat as they felt was safe. Then both of them took their diving fins and tried to fan the fires close to the ground so they would send the heat and not the smoke beneath the boat.

After a while, Jill reached in and felt Kayak's neck between his bandages and coverings ."He's not trembling so much," she said, "and his skin feels a little warmer."

"How about you?" said Matthew.

"I'm all right." Jill managed a smile. "You gave me your sweater and pushing the boat and fanning the fire have warmed me up a bit."

She reached into her packsack and took out a tin of corned beef that had lost its key. Matt cut it evenly in half with his thickest knife blade.

"Where did you learn that?" she asked.

"From him," said Matthew, nodding toward Kayak. "He's taught me almost all the useful outdoors things I know. He says he got them from his father and his grandfather. Oh, yes, and he's got lots of useful ways to do things from his grandmother as well."

Jill said, "You're lucky to have known him all this time."

"Yes, I know," said Matt. "I hope he's going to be all right," and he turned his face away from Jill, pretending to look beyond their fires. There were no sounds, no stars overhead, nothing but the moaning wind and the pitch-black night.

Kayak took only one piece of meat, though they tried to give him more.

"You want to help me roll up more tundra, before

you lie down and get some sleep?" Matt asked Jill. "I'll need a lot because I'm going to try to keep these two fires going all night for Kayak . . . and you, too," he said.

When they finished, Matt said, "Maybe you'd like to lie out of the wind between the fires and the boat. That's about the most comfortable place you'll find tonight." He paused for a moment. "I guess you'd give about anything to be back in southern California where it's warm and . . . ."

"Yes, maybe I would. But there's no point in thinking about it now. I just hope that howling wind goes somewhere else."

Beyond the lake they could hear the angry sea pounding in against the shore.

Gently, Jill felt underneath the boat. "It's warm in there," she whispered, "and I think Kayak's asleep. Rest is about the best thing for him now."

Matt laid another roll of tundra on both fires.

"Oh—that heat feels good," said Jill. "If you weren't here with me tonight, I'd be really scared."

"What are you afraid of?" asked Matthew.

"A bear, maybe," answered Jill, and she sat up and looked around. "In Yellowstone Park, they say that a fire's glow draws bears in from a long way off."

"Sometimes I think about bears, too," said Matthew, and he picked up the bang stick and pointed it out toward the darkness.

"I don't think that thing works above the water," Jill said quietly.

"What awful luck," said Jill. She knelt and spoke to Kayak. "I wish I'd had the brains to bring more food. I left the pickles and the baked beans and that big jar of peanut butter on the shelf." She offered the last hardtack biscuit to Kayak, but he was trembling so with fever that he would not eat.

Matt and Jill sat side by side, staring out at the cold gray lake.

"If this fog lasts all day," said Jill, "I'll have to admit it's worse up here than San Francisco."

"I wish we were all of us in New Mexico or Arizona, where I used to go to school," said Matt. "Arizona's warm and dry. Some parts you can go a year and never see a patch of fog."

That night, they built up their fires again, but they were so tired and hungry that they slept most of the night. When they woke, the fog had drifted off the lake and was moving out to sea.

Jill felt Kayak's head. "He's worse," she said. "And here we sit, as helpless as a caveman and his wife. To look at us you'd think that medicine had not yet been invented."

"*Iyonamut,*" gasped Kayak from beneath the boat.

"What does that mean?" Jill asked Matt.

"It means, 'It can't be helped.' Whatever is going to be is going to be. Kayak believes you can't change that."

"We would change it fast enough, if that helicopter of Charlie's would only—"

As if Jill had spoken magic words, the sound of

Matilda's engine came chopping in from the fog-hung sea. Then they saw a flash of red. *Waltzing Matilda* whirled in toward the lake. Matthew snatched off his parka and stumbled up the hill, flagging Charlie desperately as the helicopter turned away.

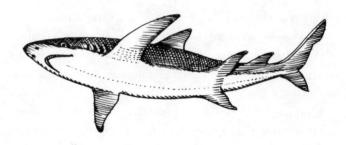

IX

THE MORNING LIGHT FLASHED AGAINST *Matilda*'s BRIGHT red sides as she turned and slowly churned through the rising mists toward them. Matt jumped up and down and yelled as loud as he could, even though he knew Charlie could not hear him above the roar of the engine. He held his parka by its sleeves, waving it like a bright blue flag. Jill waved her arms like semaphores.

When Charlie spotted them, he kept *Matilda* hovering just above them. Matt ducked down, drawing his head in like a turtle. He could see Charlie and his father sitting in the helicopter's plastic bubble. Both of them were waving down at them.

Charlie waltzed *Matilda* around in a steep, smooth curve above the upturned boat and brought her down gently and gracefully a safe thirty feet away. Then he cut the engine.

Mr. Morgan flung open the door on his side. "Are you all right?" he called. "Where's Kayak?"

"He's underneath the boat," said Jill, "and he needs to get to a hospital just as soon as you can take him there!"

The four of them carefully carried Kayak to the helicopter. Jill and Matthew quickly explained what had happened to him. Together they laid Kayak on *Matilda*'s new back seat cushions while Charlie prepared to take off again.

"Sorry," he said, "but five people are too many for this poor old kangaroo." He patted *Matilda* on the side.

"Jill should go with Kayak as his nurse," Ross Morgan said to Charlie. "You two fly Kayak to the DEW Line site and get him off to a hospital soon as you can. Matt and I will take this boat and all the diving gear back to Whale Island."

"Good thinking!" Charlie said as he helped Matt flip the long boat over and run it to the water's edge. "And here are some emergency rations for you."

"It's hard to say when we'll all see each other again," Ross Morgan said.

Jill and Charlie climbed into the helicopter and strapped Kayak into place. Then they fastened their own seat belts.

"Jill, you take good care of him for me . . . and take care of yourself," Matt called to her, as *Matilda*'s blades whirled into a silver sheen.

"Good-bye, Mattoosie," Jill called to him, using his Inuit name. "Hope I'll see you soon." Matt could see that she was crying.

Matt made no answer, for Charlie revved the engine hard, and the rotary blades lifted the helicopter into the cold August dawn. *Matilda* leveled off as she rose and swept over the low hills, heading south. Charlie was pushing the waltzer as fast as she would go toward the DEW Line site.

"I guess we've done all we could," Matt said, when they were gone. "We've got him on his way. It's up to Charlie and Jill and the doctors now."

"Kayak looked bad," Matt's father said, "but he's young and strong. He should survive this accident."

Matt and his father sat close together near the boat, broke open two of *Matilda's* emergency rations, and drank sweet lukewarm cocoa from the thermos.

"Matt," his father said, "it must have been hell for the three of you down there in the freezing water with that shark. Do you want to talk about it?"

"Not right now, Dad. Well, yes . . . maybe . . . I'm thinking about Jill. I know she could see that shark so near us, but she jumped in anyway. I couldn't have lifted Kayak up to the boat without her help."

"There's lots of men who would never have had the nerve to do what she did," Ross Morgan said.

"Kayak is like a brother to the two of us," Matt told his father. "Before we go, I'd like to pile some more rocks on this shore so Inuit carvers can find the ivory when Kayak leads them back here later."

After building the stone cairn, Matt and his father

packed their few belongings and pushed the boat out from shore.

"Most of the big mammoth tusks are right beneath us now," Matt told his father. "Kayak knows exactly where they are. Maybe we could come back next summer and help the Inuit dive for them."

Hearing the roaring of the falls, they rowed toward the entrance to the lake. They paused once while Matthew knelt cautiously on one thwart and, using Dr. Lunan's powerful binoculars, searched the center of the lake.

"He's gone," said Matt. "It's just as Kayak said. The wild man's family, his boat, everything is gone. I wanted you to meet him, Dad. He's the strange person we told you about who first led us to the gold. He likes to live alone."

"Well, this is a big country, and there's lots of space for him to move around. There are fewer humans living here than any other place on earth except Antarctica, where there are no native people, no land animals, only a handful of scientists."

When they reached the narrows between the round lake and the sea, Matt pointed out the wild man's ivory carving of a walrus. They had to pull their boat up beside the narrows and wait for a while until the tide turned and the water rose high enough to give them a smooth passage out to sea. Almost all the drifting sea ice had disappeared toward the south, and the north wind was at their back. The sea was calmer. Matt helped his father clamp the outboard engine to the stern and whirled it into life.

They raced toward Whale Island, which hung on the horizon like a dark-blue cloud.

When they were almost halfway there, Matt knelt on the thwart, then made a desperate sign for his father to cut the motor.

"What did you see?" his father asked.

"I think they were narwhals," shouted Matt.

Ross Morgan looked at the flat sea around the boat. "Are you sure?"

As if to answer him, a tusk cut the water, and a large, spotted narwhal rose not far off their bow.

"Holy cow!" Matt's father gasped. "Look at the long horn on that one."

Before Matt could speak, a second and a third narwhal blew as they broke the glassy surface of the water. Then all three humped their backs and disappeared.

"I never thought I'd really see one," said Matt's father. "Shall we try to follow them?"

"No, no," said Matthew. "Let's stop right here and be quiet. I want to see if what the Inuit believe is true."

Matt waited for about five minutes, then bending over, stared down beneath the surface. It was not long before he saw the large, spotted body of a narwhal rising up until it lay with its head beneath their boat.

"It's true, it's true!" Matt whispered. "Here comes another one."

"I can't believe it," Ross Morgan murmured, as he peered down into the water.

"Kayak says they think the white bottom of this boat is ice, and they are using it to hide from us."

After a while, each of the three narwhals rose and drew in a noisy breath of air before plunging deep into the Arctic waters.

Soon the narwhals rose to the surface again. This time there were only two large males. There, before Matthew and his father's eyes, the two great sea beasts did battle, clashing their long swordlike horns together.

"That's it!" Matthew gasped to his father. "Their horns are used for fighting, for deciding who shall have a female for its mate."

"I think you're right," his father said. "We must be among the very few who have seen them battling. Now we know how they use their ice swords."

With a great splash, the two sea unicorns disappeared beneath the surface of scattered ice.

"I'll never forget that sight in all my life," Matt's father said, as he started up the outboard motor again.

When they turned into the Whale Island landing place, Sandy Lunan and Ashevak, with Uvilu and Susee, hurried down to the cove to greet them.

"Believe me, we are glad to see you two safe and sound," Jill's father said as the group walked up to camp. "That must have been a terrible experience with the shark. I heard about it from Jill on our radio."

"It was awful," Matt said simply.

Matt noticed that Dr. Lunan moved his right arm

stiffly. He had taken it out of the plaster cast and sling.

"This morning we saw three narwhals," Matthew said. "Just as Kayak predicted, they came up right beneath our boat."

"I'm glad your father saw them," Dr. Lunan said. "I'm afraid he was beginning to think narwhals were fairy stories, or maybe like the four-footed unicorn —a myth."

"The narwhals must be on the move," said Ashevak. "They won't migrate here again until next spring.

"They were frolicking over the reefs and crowding around our observation boat when you were gone," Sandy Lunan said with pleasure. "I had a perfect chance to observe them through the bottom window. We were just about to see what they used their long tusks for," said Jill's father, "when Uvilu called that we had an urgent message on our radio. Then we heard that Charlie and Jill were at the DEW Line site and that the Mounted Police were going to fly Kayak to the hospital in Frobisher. The operator told us that you would be coming over in the boat. It's good to see you safe at last. You'll have all night to gather anything you've stored here. We're all packed and ready to go," said Dr. Lunan, as he pointed at the two snowmobiles now wrapped in heavy canvas and the pile of heavy gear and boxes in one of the only two tents left standing. "You two must be starving. Let's eat, get a sound sleep, and push off in the morning, when the tide is running in our favor. As you can see, I'm storing all the bulkiest things here under canvas, ready to set up another marine observation station next year, as I've been asked to do."

In the morning, Sandy Lunan waved good-bye to the lonely rocks that formed Whale Island. All the main ice was loose and drifting as they set out in both boats and sped toward Foxe Five. Matt imagined that he could hear the Arctic gulls and murres and small sea pigeons calling a farewell to all of them. Distant pans of ice were drifting westward on the tide, and on these flat tops Matt counted a dozen small herds of walrus lying watching them or sleeping, motionless as smooth, brown stones.

As they neared the DEW Line site, they could see beneath a bank of heavy clouds a squat, blunt-nosed cargo plane waiting on the runway. Not far away sat *Waltzing Matilda*.

Archibald McKenzie let Jill and Charlie out of his truck. They were waiting at the floating summer landing dock, watching the two boats speed in, each throwing out wide, white waves. Jill hugged her father but scarcely spoke to Matt at first. They only shook hands shyly as she did with all the others.

"The Mounted Police plane flew Kayak out of here at six last evening," Jill told them.

"We heard on the radio that they got safely into Frobisher," said Mr. McKenzie, "but now the whole east coast of Baffin Island is buried deep in fog, and the weather operator tells me he's received a severe storm warning. Ah, well, there's no use fussing. Let's be grateful that Kayak's being cared for in the hospital and that you're all here together safe and sound. Let's go find rooms for you. Your clothes look wet. You'll want to change."

Next morning, the ground was sodden, and the air was filled with driving sleet and rain. Huge, dark storm clouds rolled over the entire country, blanking out the mountains, shadowing the soggy tundra plain.

"Remember, we get a very brief summer here," Mr. McKenzie told Jill when he met her in the hallway. "One day it's light and full of alpine flowers, and the next day we have autumn coming on. This kind of storm is quite common for this time of year. It's my guess that you won't be flying east for three days, maybe four."

At breakfast, Charie announced, "Today I'm going to curl up like a duckbilled platypus and take a solid winter's nap. If the north coast weather's good, Ross Morgan can wake me, and we'll fly the long way round Baffin Island. "

Mr. Morgan turned and spoke to Matt. "Charlie's got to get *Matilda* out of here and back to Frobisher, and he can't make that trip by himself. I'll have to go along and help him wrestle with the fuel barrels and woggle in the extra gas. We'll go across the north coast first and then head south. We should be in Frobisher to greet you and Jill and Sandy when your cargo plane arrives."

"Be careful, Dad," said Matt. "We lost you and Charlie once in a storm, and I don't want it to happen again."

Matt woke early in the morning, when he heard the heavy *thunk-thunk-thunk* of *Matilda's* engine as she rose and zoomed low over the Foxe Five buildings. His father's rumpled bed was empty, and there was a quick note scribbled on a pad. It read: "See you at Frob! Love, Dad."

"Did you hear them go?" asked Matthew, when he met Jill and her father heading for the mess hall at breakfast.

"We certainly did," said Sandy Lunan. "I thought the ceiling of our room was falling in."

"An old prospector in Arizona told me once that my dad and Charlie are like a pair of circus horses. They hear the music in the distance, and they've just got to harness up and pull the painted wagon."

"Why not?" said Sandy Lunan, who was much like them himself.

Mr. McKenzie had guessed right about the weather. It was not until the fourth morning that the pilot of the cargo plane came into the mess hall carrying his maps and fully dressed to fly.

"Eat hearty, folks," he said, "then grab up all your gear. The weather's dandy here and it's C.A.V.U. at Frobisher right now."

"That means ceiling and visibility unlimited," said Dr. Lunan, "just what we need."

"We got two stops to make at other DEW Line sites," the pilot told them, "so we should get into

Frobisher sometime late this afternoon. We'll take off as soon as you can get your kit aboard."

"Good-bye, Mr. McKenzie. Thanks for everything," they called before the sturdy cargo plane rolled down the runway with a steady roar, then climbed like a flying silver hippopotamus into the cold clear Arctic sky. She was heavily loaded with boxes tied down tight, marked in French and English, PRENEZ GARDE —TRES DANGEREUX DANGEROUS—HANDLE WITH CARE. There were also bulky iron parts for broken tractors. It made Whale Island's tiny pile of freight look small.

Matthew and Jill stared out the window, watching the low coastal plain join the shadowy blue mountains.

"This is a hard country," Matthew said, "but somehow I feel that I belong here. It has come to seem like home to me."

"Why?" asked Jill.

"Maybe it's because I don't have a real home anywhere else," said Matthew. "But mostly I think it's because of Kayak. He calls himself my brother, and I feel the same way about him," said Matt. "I hope he's getting better."

"Me, too," said Jill. "I miss him and the warm way he smiles. I was born in the sunshine of southern California, and I never thought I'd learn to live in Arctic cold and like it. But now, just looking out over this huge island and those peaceful mountains wrapped in pure white snow . . ." Jill had tears in her eyes when she said, "I hate leaving . . . not knowing if I'll ever again see you or Kayak or Ashevak or your dad or Uvilu and Susee."

"I hope you will," said Matt. "Now that we three have become like a family, kind of . . . it would be terrible if we never got together again."

"I can't even think of that," said Jill, as she got up from the seat beside him. "There's no hostess on this plane, so I'm going to pass the biscuits and thermos jug of coffee to the pilot, the copilot, and my dad. Here, take this cup," she said to Matt, not looking at him. "You can be . . . my first customer."

"Thanks, Jill." Matt heard the pilot laugh. "A grand girl like you in a parka as beautiful as that one would be welcome to fly with us—forever."

They landed briefly on two remote airstrips and threw off cargo and then they were in the air again, headed for Frobisher Bay.

An hour after the last stop, the pilot called back, "Fasten your seat belts, friends. We'll be landing any minute."

Matt's watch said 4:21. He looked out the window at the colorful scattering of rooftops at Apex, where Kayak lived, and the long, narrow, curving road that connected it with Frobisher. He could see the airfield, the control tower, and beyond it the huge U.S. military building. He proudly pointed out to Jill his doughnut-shaped school building that shone below them like a silver spaceship.

The stubby cargo plane began her final approach. Matt strained against his seat belt, trying to see *Matilda*. She should have been sitting by the airstrip on the helicopter pad, bright red against the newly-fallen snow. If *Matilda* wasn't there, she wasn't any-

where in Frobisher. Matt thought of the violent storm
that they had avoided over central Baffin. I hope,
he prayed, we haven't lost the two of them again.

"Is anything the matter?" Jill asked him.

"I was just hoping Dad and Charlie were okay.
They haven't landed here." As he said those words,
the wheels of the heavy cargo plane made a touch-
down that was smooth as silk. "Now keep your
fingers crossed," Matt told her. "All we want to hear
is that Kayak's well again and my dad and Charlie
are somewhere safe and sound."

When the plane stopped, the copilot hurried back
and pushed open the wide freight door. "Don't
worry, we'll take off all your gear."

"I'll help," said Dr. Lunan, flexing his stiff arm.

Jill jumped down onto the slippery airstrip and
Matt followed her. They ran toward the hangar and
pulled open the door of the overheated waiting room.

"Are you Jill Lunan from the Whale Island Research Station?" the young Mounted Policeman asked
her.

"Yes, I am," Jill answered.

"They want you and your father to weigh in all
your luggage and your freight at the Nordair counter
right away. There's a plane flying south to Montreal
this evening. It's the only one this week or next that
has enough space to take all your party and equipment. Your other divers have just arrived from Cape
Dorset. That means you've got lots of strong arms
ready to organize the freight."

"Thank you," said Jill. "I'll tell my father."

"And you must be Matthew Morgan." The young policeman shook his hand. "My name is Peter." He opened the side door and pointed at the four-wheel drive. "Jump in," he said. "I'm here to give you a ride."

"I hope you're taking us to see Kayak," Matthew told him.

"Good guess," the policeman said. "They moved him out of the hospital this morning. His family wanted to have him home, so the nurse has agreed to go up to Apex and see him every day."

At that moment, Jill's father came into the waiting room, and she gave him the message.

"We won't be long," said Jill, "but I can't leave here without seeing Kayak."

"You two say good-bye for me while I check the baggage," said Sandy Lunan. "I hope he's feeling better."

The police jeep took the road around the edge of Frobisher through the rolling, treeless hills to Apex and skidded to a stop on a patch of ice in front of Kayak's house.

"I'll leave you here," said Peter. "I know how anxious Kayak is to see you both."

"Can you find out anything about my father and Charlie? They should be here by now."

"I'll check with the flight tower on that," Peter said, "then come back to pick you up."

Matt pushed open the outer plywood door and went inside the porch that was partly painted bright lime-green. There were two rifles, a huge coil of frayed rope, a roll of winter caribou skins, a battered Primus stove, and a large fresh-killed seal lying on the floor. He knocked on the inner door.

A man's voice called, "*Eteree*—come in."

Matt opened the second door and heard Kayak's voice. "I've been lying here thinking, will they both come and see me or will Jill have to run onto that airplane too fast and fly straight home to Sandy-Aggooo?"

"Do I seem like a girl who would go away without saying good-bye to you?" Jill asked.

"No." Kayak tried to laugh through the clean white bandages that still covered his neck and chest and more than half his face.

Jill and Matthew smiled and shook hands with Kayak's family—his father, his mother, his grandmother, and his sister, Pia, and his big dog, Shulu—before they sat down on the side of Kayak's bed.

"You can say anything you want in English," Kayak said, "because my folks don't understand that language. Except Pia, she understands quite a bit, but she never tells a word."

"How are you?" Jill asked him.

"I'm feeling lots better," Kayak told them. "I didn't like being in the hospital. But I feel good now that I'm at home with all my family. They're giving me all the fresh seal meat and caribou and fish that I can eat.

"Jill," Kayak said, "when they first took me into

the hospital, they changed my bandages. I saw you had torn up your great-uncle's shirt for me."

"It was only an old shirt," said Jill. "It didn't matter. What does matter is that you're alive and that you're getting better."

"I tried to have them save the bandages, but they threw most of them away. All I've got is this one." He held up a small torn strip with the words, NAVY DIVE. "My mother washed it for you." He held it out to Jill.

"No, you keep it for good luck," she said. "I want it to remind you of all the wonderful times that we three have had together."

"My mom was right. She said you wouldn't go away without saying good-bye to me, so she's been working hard. She made you a new pair of sealskin mitts with a pair of loons sewn on for luck because you're a diver. That's white-fox fur around the wrists. You can say *nakoamee*—that's thanks—to her if you want, but don't tell her that it's too hot where you are living to wear fur mitts."

"Oh, they are so beautiful," said Jill, and she started to cry and went and hugged Kayak's mother and Pia.

"My mother says she thinks you were very brave to go diving down near that *ikhaloojuak*—that means 'big shark.' My father says he can teach me to hunt, but he doesn't know a single Inuk who can teach me to go diving underneath the ice. He says he wouldn't mind if I went to school to learn from those who go down there. He wants me to learn to use that bang stick right."

Even as Kayak was telling them what his father had said, they heard the *thug-thug-thug* of a helicopter cutting in, through the early autumn twilight.

Matthew ran to the small window, then laid his forehead gratefully against the ice-cold glass. "Oh, thank God. There she is!" he cried. "It's my dad and Charlie. They're coming in. I can see *Matilda*'s lights flashing. They're coming home!"

The young policeman, Peter, came and opened the door. He smiled at Kayak's family. "Sorry, but there's not much time," he said. "Jill and her father have to fly out to Montreal tonight."

Kayak started to get out of bed, but Pia stopped him. "The doctor made me promise to stay in bed for one whole week," Kayak explained. "He said that Pia was going to be my other nurse—so she can boss me!"

Pia smiled at Jill, who bent over and kissed Kayak on his unbandaged cheek.

"You've got to stay in bed and take good care of yourself for me," Jill said. "I hate to say it, but I've got to go. There's a French word, *à bientôt*, that doesn't mean good-bye. It just means—until I see you again."

"I like that," said Kayak. But when he tried to say *ahh-bee-an-tow* to Jill, he got the word all twisted up and in the end, he put up his hands to hide his face. Matthew could see that he was weeping.

"Mattoosie," Kayak said in a shaky voice. "Don't you go away from me right now. I got more things I got to say to you."

"Don't worry—I'm staying right here with you," said Matt.

Jill wiped her eyes with her new mitts, then hurried out of the little plywood house. Kayak's family went out to say good-bye to her as she climbed into the backseat of the policeman's jeep. Matthew came out a few minutes later, and the three of them drove down the long hill to the airport without saying a single word.

Matthew pointed to the pad where *Waltzing Matilda* was resting by the runway. "Thanks a lot for the ride," he said, as they got out of the jeep.

"Here she comes," said Peter. "The Nordair flight is right on time."

They watched the sleek, wide-bodied silver jet as her pilot let down the wheels, set the wing flaps, and prepared to land. Matt and Jill looked at each other, but neither could think of any words to say. They went inside the airport's waiting room and gathered up Jill's backpack, which they had left behind the counter.

Dr. Lunan came in, followed by half a dozen strong young men, each carrying brightly painted boxes, oxygen tanks, aluminum trunks, and bulky duffle bags.

Jill and her father introduced each one of them to Matthew. "This is our other diving team," said Dr. Lunan. "They've just flown over from Cape Dorset."

"Have you seen my dad or Charlie?" Matt asked Jill's father.

"Yes, I saw them just a minute ago. They're still bringing equipment from the helicopter. I sent one of our divers to help them."

When the door swung open, Matthew darted over to greet Charlie and his father. "Oh, I'm glad to see you back! What took you so long?" Matt asked.

"You know your dad," said Charlie. "He can't fly anywhere without setting down and tapping rocks with that sharp-nosed hammer of his. Just look at all that underwater hardware." Charlie laughed. "Being a prospector is a lot like being a scuba diver. They both carry too much stuff. In the Outback of Australia, some native chaps I used to know wandered about all winter without a single stitch of clothing on. . . . Where's that Jill? We can't let her get away without saying good-bye to me and your old man, too."

Jill hugged them both. "Thank you," she said. "I hope I'll see you . . . next . . . well, sometime . . . maybe." She turned away. "Matt, let's go outside for a minute. It's getting awfully hot in here."

Jill and Matt stood together in the gathering gloom. She shivered. "School is starting soon. I wonder. . . ."

The airport loudspeaker crackled into life and a man's thick voice said, "Nordair Flight #7 for Monteral is now ready for boarding. *Numéro sept destiné à Montréal est maintenant prêt.*"

The door swung open and a dozen passengers, all

men in bulky Arctic parkas, filed out across the
runway to the waiting aircraft.

"I have nothing to give you," Jill," said Matthew,
"but Kayak wanted me to give you this."

"I can't take that," said Jill. "It's his knife—the
one his grandfather gave him."

"He told me to tell you thanks for giving your best
shirt to him. He wants you to have his knife." He
pressed it into her hand. "I wish I had something to
give you."

"You already have, Mattoosie. You and Kayak just
gave me the best summer of my life."

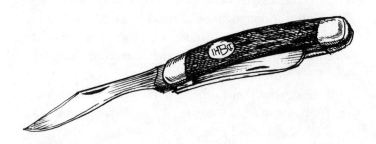

X

"MATT, JILL, LISTEN TO THIS. I'VE GOT GOOD NEWS," said Dr. Lunan as he came toward them waving a radiogram. "The director in San Diego says they developed the rolls of film we sent south and he believes they are the best narwhal photographs ever taken. The director wants Jill to come north with us again next year."

"That's wonderful news," said Matthew. "I was worried that I might not see Jill again."

"Oh, we'll be back," her father said. "And Matt, I want to thank you and Kayak for helping me while I had this broken arm. Without you two, Jill never would have been able to take all those underwater narwhal photographs."

Matt glanced at Jill, who seemed not to be listening. She was staring far across Frobisher Bay at the September mountains already white with snow.

"Good-bye, Matthew." Dr. Lunan shook his hand, then hurried toward the other divers who were boarding the waiting plane.

Jill could hardly bring herself to say good-bye.

"A *bientôt*, Mattoosie," she said almost in a whisper, then quickly slung her pack across her back and ran toward the plane.

Matt had a lonely feeling as he watched Jill climb the steps and disappear inside. The flight attendant closed the heavy metal door, and two airport workers rolled the boarding ramp away. One by one, the four big jet engines whined into life as the long, sleek plane rolled slowly down the runway.

In one bright window over the wing of the plane, Matt saw a pair of diver's flippers waving to him. He waved back as the plane gained speed for takeoff, then rose into the air. He watched it move against the snow-capped mountains until its wing lights disappeared. At that moment, the Arctic seemed the loneliest place in the world.

Matthew still felt very glum when he went inside and found Charlie and his father waiting for him.

"Matt, before we tell you all our news, I'd like to ask you something. Where would you like to go to school this year?"

"It's good right here in Frobisher," Matt said. "And best of all, it gives me a chance to see Kayak every day."

"You could go here," his father said, "or somewhere else."

"If I were to change from Frobisher, I'd kind of

like to go to school down south, you know, some
place, like, maybe, San Diego. I could study there
and take extra courses in geology and marine biology.
They teach diving down there."

Charlie smiled and put his arm around Matt's
shoulders. "How soon do you want to go, old beano?"

"Oh, I don't know," said Matt. "I could be ready
for tomorrow's plane."

"No," said Charlie. "That's too soon. The doctor
says Kayak can't go with you unless you wait a week."

"Kayak come with me?" said Matthew. "Holy
smoke! Having Kayak with me would be about the
best thing in the world. He's never even see a tree,
and he'll go bonkers when Jill takes him to that zoo.
I wonder what he'll think of San Diego and the warm
Pacific Ocean? Could we take him down to Mexico?"

"I guess you could." Ross Morgan smiled at his
son. "You step right over here to this ticket agent
and we'll ask him to write up two return tickets—
one for you and one for Kayak."

"Wait, Dad. Those two tickets will cost an awful
lot of money"

"Now"—Charlie laughed with glee—"this brings
us to the good part of what your father's got to tell
you. Speak quietly," Charlie warned Ross Morgan.
"These plywood walls have ears."

They looked around the almost-empty airport, then
chose the farthest corner, where the overhead light
was strong.

"Sit down, Matt," his father said, as he rummaged
through his well-worn shoulder bag and drew out

two large pieces of white quartz. He held the first one up for Matt's inspection.

His father didn't have to say a word, for Matt could plainly see the rich, thick vein of gold that curved like a yellow river through the white-quartz sample.

"Phew!" Matt gasped. "I never saw anything as rich as that, unless it was in rock collection of the Smithsonian Museum in Washington."

"That's only half the good news." Charlie chuckled. "Are you ready for the second? Your dad and I landed old *Matilda* and then we walked along that white-quartz fault. It's almost a whole mile long," he whispered.

"Charlie's right." Matt's father whistled with delight. "We picked rich samples all the way. I brought this one to show you what it looked like at the other end." He held up a second quartz sample with a dozen rich gold veins running through it like the branches of a tree.

"Your old man and I worked like a pair of beavers. We've got most of it staked already."

"So," Ross Morgan continued, "don't you and Kayak worry about the cost of those two tickets, son. I radioed Jill's father, and he promised that if you did go to school in San Diego, he'd keep a careful eye on you and Kayak and find a proper place for both of you to live."

"Dad, are you and Charlie going to stay up here?"

"Yes. Don't worry about us. We'll keep busy enough attending to our new claims. This is one gold mine that's not going to slip away from us. Why, Charlie might even buy a brand-new helicopter and turn in poor old *Waltzing*—"

"Hold on a minute, chum," said Charlie. "I never said a horrid thing like that. Don't you forget, Ross Morgan, without *Matilda* we never would have found that great long vein of gold. I'm going to give her a shiny set of rotary blades and a bushel of new parts for Christmas. When *Matilda* does grow tired of fly-ing, I'm going to let her rest forever in the Yellow-knife Museum."

"Speaking of Christmas," said Matt's father, "Charlie says he'll fly down with me to San Diego for the holidays so you and Kayak won't get lonely. How does that sound?"

Matt smiled as he reached in his pocket and set Kayak's lucky stone on top of the two gold samples. "It sounds to me," said Matt, "as though all of us have struck the best luck in the world."